WAYLON GODDAMN JENNINGS

Buddy Holly was his mentor. Johnny Cash was his roommate. And today, he and his wife Jessi Colter seem to have a storybook marriage.

But if Waylon Jennings's life has been touched by stardust, it's also been plagued by tragedy, frustration, drug abuse, and the threat of bankruptcy.

Waylon Jennings has seen it all. But with each setback, he dug himself out of the rubble and started over again the only way he knew how — with his music.

And somehow, along the way, he became a country music legend.

WAYLON JENNINGS

WAYLON JENNINGS

by Albert Cunniff

ZEBRA BOOKS

KENSINGTON PUBLISHING CORP.

ZEBRA BOOKS

are published by

Kensington Publishing Corp.
475 Park Avenue South
New York, NY 10016

First printing: December 1985

Printed in the United States of America

Cover photo by Raeanne Rubenstein, 1985
– –TELEPHOTO

Table of Contents

Author's Note

I appreciate the direction I received from Waylon Jennings's staff and advisers. As always, thanks to the staff of the Country Music Foundation Library and Media Center in Nashville for their service and suggestions.

I refer to these books in my work: *Lost Highway*, by Peter Guralnick, Vintage Books, New York, 1979; *The Outlaws: Revolution in Country Music,* by Michael Bane, Doubleday/Dolphin, New York, 1978; *Country Music: White Man's Blues,* by John Grissim, Paperback Library, New York, 1970; and *The Buddy Holly Story,* by John Goldrosen, Quick Fox, New York, 1979. Some quotes from Waylon and Jessi, unless otherwise cited, are from artist biographies released by their respective labels.

This book is dedicated to my wife Norma for her patience, Susan Moffat for her referral, and Albert Cunniff Sr. and Phyllis Cunniff for their love.

Albert Cunniff
Nashville, Tennessee
December, 1985

Chapter One

Waylon Goddamn Jennings

Waylon Jennings was ready to quit the music business for the first time in mid-February, 1959.

Waylon, twenty-one, was in New York, preparing to join three friends in a long drive back to Lubbock, Texas, after completing a physically and emotionally gruelling six-week winter concert tour. The tour had brought the death of Waylon's friend and mentor, Buddy Holly, who had died in a plane crash just two weeks earlier. It had also brought Waylon's first experience with unscrupulous booking agents, his first experience with amphetamines, and his own brush with death—Waylon had traded places with one of the men who accompanied Buddy on the plane.

During the trip home the engine of the 1958 Chevy they drove burned out somewhere in Missouri. It was an appropriate symbol, as Waylon was also feeling pretty burned out—he'd had all he could stomach of the music business.

Waylon Jennings's life has been unusual by almost anyone's standards. He knows what it's like to earn $50,000 for a night's show—and what it's like to be

$2 million in debt. He has six children by four marriages. He suffered through twenty-one years of drug abuse and court battles, and fought for more than a decade against record labels that wanted to change him and his music.

Along the way Waylon became a living country music legend, largely through such songs as "Are You Sure Hank Done It This Way," "Luckenbach, Texas," "I've Always Been Crazy," "Good Hearted Woman," and a dozen gold and platinum albums, including *Wanted! The Outlaws, Greatest Hits, I've Always Been Crazy, Dreaming My Dreams,* and more.

Jennings was one of the prime figures in country music's "outlaw" movement in the mid-1970s, and is recognized today for having opened the door with his struggles for other country artists to gain more control over their music and careers. Still, Nashville's music industry has never been sure how to take Waylon. He remains what *New York Daily News* writer Bill Bell calls "the ornery but sensitive barbarian outside the gates of the Grand Ole Opry, more country than most stars inside" (February 3, 1985).

His role as The Storyteller on TV's "Dukes of Hazzard," an occasional crossover record, two Grammys, numerous gold and platinum records, and other achievements have earned him a wide group of fans. They know that with Waylon you don't get traditional country, contemporary country, rockabilly, or country-rock—you get Waylon music.

Waylon's accomplishments have, however, been offset by disillusionment and emotional burnout that made him feel like quitting the music business on several occasions:

—After Holly's death in February 1959.

—When Waylon, sick with hepatitis and drug

addiction, was near bankruptcy in 1972.

— When he was near bankruptcy again and still heavily addicted to drugs in 1980.

— And in early 1983, when his financial and music business worries were over, but he was bored and depressed, and his drug addiction had become life-threatening.

More than once Waylon has had to dig himself out of the rubble and start all over, making a living the only way he knows how — with his music.

Waylon is a charismatic figure, a tall, dark Texan with rugged good looks. He stands six-one and a half, weighing over 200 pounds (especially since kicking drugs in 1984), with dark brown hair and light brown eyes that peer solemnly out from under a black, felt-rimmed hat.

A black fringe beard leaves exposed his lined cheeks, which curve in like the pinched crown of a fedora. He has dark, somewhat greasy-looking shoulder-length hair, and often sports gold and turquoise chains around his neck, a black tooled-leather vest, pointy-toed black cowboy boots, and jeans.

When Waylon is serious his face, etched with lines from years of rowdy living, reflects a surprising sensitivity which catches those who don't know him off guard.

He looks and has been known to act like the rebel he has extolled in his songs since gaining control of his music in the early 1970s. A tough-looking dude, he looks like the sort of friend you want on your side in a saloon brawl.

Waylon has a sense of humor about the macho, Big Bad John image that many male country singers cultivate. He's a tough man who finds it easy to show tenderness and understanding, and who has no qualms about telling a fellow man, "I love you."

Beneath his rough exterior is a man who genuinely cares about the human race—especially the underprivileged. Waylon gets a lump in his throat when he learns through the newspaper or TV news of someone's misfortune, and often has helped someone out with money or a good deed, offered anonymously.

He is a complex man who lives by simple values, an artist whose real turn-on is not fame and wealth, but performing, recording, and writing music with what he calls "soul."

Waylon Jennings is not an easy personality to pin down. He is articulate and reticent, warm and sardonic, unpolished and artistic, tough-skinned and vulnerable. His free-wheeling views and actions led one music critic to describe him as "part cowboy, part biker."

Waylon Jennings, along with Willie Nelson, represents perhaps the greatest force in the movement away from orchestrated blandness in country music and toward a vibrant, gritty, more personalized sound. His stylized country-rock sound acknowledges the influence of such founding fathers of country music as Hank Williams and Jimmie Rodgers, but refuses to compromise with Nashville's slick, commercial sound.

Everything he sings is totally real and comes from within. Waylon has a distinctive, gruff voice that has different qualities in different ranges, reaching a near-growl, sounding like it was distilled in charcoal, then shifting abruptly into an eerie tenor.

His views and attitudes were shaped by experience, not image-makers Waylon is real.

New York City, late 1972
Max's Kansas City nightclub

Waylon is on stage at Max's, to open his show at
this pop club in a city not familiar with him or his
music. He is weak from a recent bout with hepatitis
and is in the throes of drug addiction, but his career
is finally shifting into high gear after more than
thirteen years of hard work.

Waylon introduces his band to the audience and is
ready to begin a song, when a woman's voice shouts
from somewhere out in the darkness, "And who the
hell are you?"

Waylon peers out through the stage lights and his
face cracks into a crooked grin as he answers,
"Waylon — Goddamn — Jennings, Lady."

Chapter Two

"You'll Do Anything to Get Out of West Texas"

In 1937 *Newsweek* and *Look* magazines published their first issues . . . America's business economy, which had been recovering from the Depression over the past few years, took a sharp turn for the worse . . . the first Bugs Bunny cartoon hit movie theaters — and Waylon Jennings was born.

Wayland Arnold Jennings was born on June 15, 1937, to William Alvin and Lorene Jennings in the West Texas town of Littlefield, which Waylon likes to describe as "a suburb to a cotton patch." Located about a hundred miles south of Amarillo and thirty miles northwest of Lubbock, Littlefield (population 6,700) is surrounded by small towns with such picturesque names as Muleshoe, Circle Back, Whiteface, Shallowater, and Sundown.

The land around Littlefield is flat and open, like much of West Texas's plains land. Still, there must be something in the soil or water that encourages musical creativity, because an amazing number of music greats have come from West Texas. In fact the Littlefield/Lubbock area itself has given us such stars as

Buddy Holly, Mac Davis, Roy Orbison, Don Williams, Waylon Jennings, and others.

"It's kind of like they say sports is with black dudes, it's a way to get up and away from something that's bad," Waylon said (*Popular Music and Society*, No. 3, 1974). "You'll do anything to get out of West Texas."

Waylon says his first name came from combining Wade and Gaylon. "My grandmother, when she was young, her boyfriend's name was Wade, and I was [her] first grandchild. She wanted to name me Wade, and Mama wanted to name me Gaylon, and Daddy wanted me to have W. A. for initials 'cause it's a traditional [family] thing" (*Country Music*, April 1981).

The baby's name was originally Wayland, but his mother changed that when a Baptist minister visited her the day after she gave birth and said, "I see you named your son after our school." It turns out that there's a Wayland Baptist University in Plainview, about fifty miles northeast of Littlefield. Lorene Jennings, a dyed-in-the-wool Church of Christ believer, lost no time in changing Wayland's name to its current spelling.

As an infant Waylon rejected his mother's breast milk and became so ill that his mother, fearing he would soon die, made sure to have a picture taken holding her son so that she'd have something to remember him by.

On July 8, 1938, Lorene gave birth to Tommy Jennings. There would be two more Jennings sons, James D. and youngest son Bo.

W. A. Jennings, Waylon's father, was a god-fearing (Church of Christ) truck-driving man in Littlefield. W. A. played guitar and harmonica in a local band for a while, and after a hard day's work he often pulled out his guitar at home and played some old Jimmie Rodgers tunes or folk songs.

Times were tough for the Jennings family. Waylon's mother cleaned the homes of a few wealthy families in the area to earn extra money. W. A. broke his back around 1939, when Waylon was two, and picked cotton while he was still in a cast to earn nine dollars to buy the family Christmas presents. Later, W. A. got his own truck and earned a living hauling goods for a couple of years, managing to save enough money to start a feed store.

"I can remember helping to shovel grain out of the truck," Waylon said. "We'd go to what they called 'wheat harvests' and we'd go buy fruit and vegetables, sell them and then, too, Dad would go buy watermelons from East Texas. I would sit on the depot lot and sell them. I wasn't much bigger than knee-high to a grasshopper" (*Music City News*, May 1966).

"I remember some hard times, but I think I remember a whole lot more good times in simple ways.

". . . [M]y Dad was the greatest man I'll ever know—and he never really succeeded in any type of business. Every time he got into something, it seemed like it went wrong. He failed in several kinds of businesses, but he was the most successful man I've ever known. . . ." (*Record & Radio Mirror*, February 16, 1974).

When Waylon was about seven his grandfather had a cafe, and Waylon loved to go there and listen to the jukebox, then still called a "nickelodeon." He'd slip out behind the restaurant with two uncles who were his age, and they'd each pretend to be their favorite country singer from the Grand Ole Opry. Picking at a broken broom stick that served as his guitar, Waylon tried to sing like Ernest Tubb. "I made Hank

Williams sound pop," he later joked.

On Friday nights Waylon's dad hooked the truck up to the battery-powered radio, and the Jennings family had a big ol' time listening to country music.

"The first country music I remember hearing was the Grand Ole Opry. There wasn't a lot of country radio up in that part of Texas in those days. Saturday night was about it . . .

"There was a blind fella—I can't remember his name—had a two-hour program out of Levelland. We'd hear the Carter Family on Friday night and the Grand Ole Opry on Saturday. Daddy pulled the truck up to the window and hooked the radio up to the truck battery. I'd be sittin' around that old pot-bellied stove with my dad. He liked Bill Monroe. He'd hear that come on, and he'd just sit there and grin (*Dallas Times Herald*, November 13, 1983).

Young Waylon was influenced by the music of such country stars of the day as Ernest Tubb, Carl Smith, Webb Pierce, Little Jimmy Dickens, Hank Williams, and Bob Wills. The family radio also picked up radio station KWKH from Shreveport, Louisiana, and this gave Waylon an early exposure to the blues, via such artists as B. B. King, Bobby "Blue" Bland, and Jimmy Reed.

Waylon recalls first taking an interest in the guitar at age four. W. A. and Lorene both played guitar, and each one taught him a bit about their style. Waylon's dad had a Gene Autry guitar with scenes of the Old West painted on it. His parents gave Waylon his first guitar—a Gibson that was "bowed like a bow and arrow"—when he was about ten. Lorene pulled cotton to earn $5 to buy it. Waylon proceeded to drive everyone in his house to distraction with his incessant guitar playing.

One Christmas when things were going a bit better for the Jennings family, Waylon got a nicer guitar, a Harmony, and his brother Tommy got a mandolin, which he never bothered to learn how to play. (Tommy did learn to play the bass, though, and later played that instrument in Waylon's band.)

When Waylon was eleven his father ran a produce business, buying eggs and cream and selling feed at his store. Waylon's job was washing the cream cans, but more often than not he could be found practicing guitar while sitting on feed sacks, or on the bench that was supposedly reserved for customers to relax on.

At age twelve, in 1949, he felt confident enough to enter a local radio talent show, KSEL's "Saturday Jamboree," with his friend Bill Pollard, also twelve. The Jamboree was hosted by W. J. "Hi-Pockets" Duncan, a DJ who enjoyed featuring amateur talent, and whose career would again cross paths with Waylon's in years to come. By the time he was thirteen Waylon had his own band, the Texas Longhorns, with whom he entered — and won — many local talent shows.

Jennings and Pollard were playing a box-supper affair one afternoon when they caught the ear of a local entrepreneur who owned a newspaper and radio station. He was impressed with the boys, and offered them their own 15-minute show on radio station KVOW on Sunday mornings. Waylon admitted that having his own show "liked to scare me to death." First he and Pollard just sang and played guitars — later Waylon started to spin records, too. He didn't get paid at KVOW: "Oh, no. I would have paid them in those days!"

"I remember one time I was trying to learn two songs before the show — Webb Pierce's 'My Heart

18

Belongs to Me' and Carl Smith's 'Are You Teasing Me'—and I got so scared that I sang the words of one to the melody of the other" (*Country Music: White Man's Blues*, Grissim).

Waylon has fond memories of family singalongs that lasted well past midnight. Once his parents arranged for him to take lessons, but that only lasted about two weeks. "The teacher was showing me how to work my hand around the neck, which I already knew because I'd been playing for three or four years, and I figured this ain't gonna work" (*Guitar Player*, January 1984).

Waylon's infatuation with the cowboy life and mythology took root one day in the late 1940s, when he went to the local movie theater to see a personal appearance of Lash LaRue, the whip-cracking silver screen cowboy hero: "After they showed the movie, Lash got up on the stage and was doin' these whip tricks for the audience, and he accidentally tore a hole in the movie screen. Later, I went into the lobby to get some popcorn, and there was Lash, still carryin' his gun and his whip.

"They were tellin' him he was gonna have to pay for the movie screen, and he said he wouldn't—that they shoulda had insurance. They kept sayin', 'You're gonna pay for it!' And finally, he just said, 'I got a whip and a gun here that says I ain't!' " (*Genesis*, December 1984).

KVOW had block-style music programming that was popular at many radio stations in those days: fifteen minutes of this and fifteen minutes of that, the Hillbilly Hit Parade, pop standards, Music From Dixieland, Montovani . . . Waylon was delighted when he finally convinced the station's owner to let him play two hours of country music in the afternoon. This was the start of a seven-year stretch of radio work for Waylon at stations in Littlefield, Lubbock, and later, Phoenix.

Waylon wrote his first song, "Big Time Ladies Man," around age fourteen. Eight years later he sold it for $20 to satisfy a debt.

Waylon's stage outfit included a cowboy suit, white Stetson hat, the obligatory cowboy boots, and an f-hole guitar. "The first time that I ever went out on a stage (around 1951) and actually realized I was performing for people was on a show that starred Billy Walker, Jimmy and Johnny, Tillman Franks, and I don't know, somebody else.

". . . I did a Faron Young song. 'If You Ain't Lovin' Then You Ain't Livin',' and I got halfway through it and lost my voice, liked to choke to death, on top of a nervous bustdown. That was my first experience on stage, and it almost ended the whole thing" (*Country Song Roundup*, March 1975).

By the late 1950s Waylon was playing guitar and singing on KLLL-Lubbock's "Sunday Dance Party," another amateur talent show. ". . . I have some tapes from a KLLL radio show in 1956 where I was playing lead . . . I found I was paying the lead players more than I was paying myself. Finally, I learned to play in front of people, and there I was doing it" (*Guitar Player*, January 1984).

Waylon's music involvements interested him a whole lot more than the classes he was taking at Littlefield's high school. "I went to about middle ways of the tenth grade. I goofed off for a year after that, then went into music—it's what I always wanted to do" (*Door*, December 9–23, 1971).

Waylon picked cotton, worked for his father, who still had the feed store, and for a short time even drove a cement truck—though that job ended when he overturned the truck and permanently cemented someone's front yard. Waylon and his small band were also playing amateur radio shows and theaters around Littlefield whenever they got the chance. Waylon got an early exposure to rhythm-and-blues music. "I used to hang out in black nightclubs. I was the only white dude they'd let in there" (*Houston Chronicle*, September 7, 1975).

Waylon and his friends took to the small notoriety that their music afforded them. There wasn't much to do around Littlefield, so they turned up their collars, put on black cowboy hats, nailed taps to the heels of their boots, and kicked up sparks as they walked down Main Street.

In 1955 life took a more serious turn for Waylon when he married Maxine Lawrence on December 24. Maxine, originally from Dinuba, California, lived at the time in Spade, Texas, a tiny town ten miles east of Littlefield. Waylon had met her at a local beauty contest that he and his band entertained at, and which Maxine had entered.

Waylon and Maxine were both eighteen when they got married. They traveled sixty miles across the New Mexico border to Clovis, where they were married before Waylon's brother Tommy and Lorene Jennings, who signed a form verifying that Waylon was over eighteen. Thinking Maxine was pregnant, "We got married at 3 p.m. and at 8 we found out she wasn't," Waylon said.

Though Waylon and Maxine would have three children together and remain married for seven years, theirs was not a union made in heaven. They often fought, mostly over Waylon's career versus his marriage, and money was always in short supply.

Waylon admits his mind wasn't on being the best father or husband in those days. Still, he worked hard to support his family, at various times serving as a yard bird and bookkeeper in a lumber yard, delivering freight, pulling cotton, selling men's wear, and working in a grocery store. "I haven't had it too bad, though, compared to a lot of people. Work never did hurt anybody, y'know" (*Music City News*, May 1966).

Around 1954 he met Lubbock native and fellow struggling musician Buddy Holly. ". . . [W]e played a lot of those shows together, Buddy and his band, I had my band, a different theater every Saturday afternoon. Sometimes the same band would win it two or three weeks running. We were still playing country — Buddy, too — hell, there wasn't anything else, really.

"I saw Elvis Presley in 1955, I guess it was, in Lubbock. Well, it changed things in a way. I think it changed Buddy, too, at least I think it had a bearing. Actually it changed almost everything, really. Country music almost died at that time. Rock 'n roll killed off just about everything. It was like an explosion, definitely, you know it was actually like that" (*Lost Highway*, Guralnick).

Waylon and Maxine's first child, a boy named Terry Vance Jennings, was born on January 21, 1957. Their second child, Julie Rae, was born on August 12, 1958. By then Waylon had moved to Lubbock, where he had a job as a DJ at country radio station KLLL.

He continued to perform and write music. In his mind, radio was a "stepping stone" to the career as a singer that he really wanted. The first of his compositions to be recorded was "Young Widow Brown," which Frankie Miller cut in 1958.

"About as far back as I can remember, all I ever wanted to be was a singer. At one time I tried to be a preacher. My mother wanted one of her four boys to

22

be a preacher, but that didn't work at all, 'cause all I ever wanted to be was a singer. If I couldn't be a singer, I think I would be connected in some way with some crazy business . . . like this business . . ." (*Country Song Roundup*, March 1975).

Chapter Three

"I Was Buddy Holly's Protege"

"If he hadn't given up his charter-flight seat to a friend back in February 1959, Waylon Jennings might be known to the world only as an accident statistic."

— *Playboy*, October 1973

Waylon grew up listening to the music of Hank Williams and George Jones, but like most teenagers of his day, he found a new excitement in the music of Buddy Holly and other rockabilly artists.

Hi-Pockets Duncan was promoting concerts and helping rising young talent. He had "Saturday Jamboree" morning show on KSEL-Lubbock. Twelve-year-old Waylon and friend Bill Pollard played that show around 1949, winning first prize.

That show would lead to Duncan later introducing Waylon to Buddy Holly. Later, Waylon, in addition to working as a DJ, was also performing in the Lubbock area.

Hi-Pockets left KSEL in September 1953 to join

KDAV-Lubbock, which Dave "Pappy" Stone (David Pinkston) had just formed, and which is now considered the first all-country radio station in America. Though KDAV was a country station, it featured rock as well, on a "Rock 'n Roll Hit Parade" segment. Duncan also transferred his local talent show from KSEL, changing its name and day. Thus the "Saturday Jamboree" became KDAV's "Sunday Dance Party."

The country/bluegrass trio of Buddy, Bob & Larry that became a favorite on this show included Bob Montgomery, Larry Welburn—and a local teenager named Buddy Holly. Sonny Curtis also performed occasionally with Holly's group.

"I'd known Buddy since 1954," Waylon recalled. "We got started on a program they called the 'Sunday Dance Party' on a radio station (KDAV) in Lubbock. Every Sunday they'd let all the local yokels get out there and sing on Sunday afternoons for nothing at intermissions during the Country Music shows that would come to town . . .

"We worked a lot of shows together, them as one act and me as another" (*Country Music People*, July 1971).

Waylon was still attending high school in Littlefield when he met Holly at KDAV. "All afternoon you got to go up there and play for nothin' except the exposure, which we wouldn't miss for nothing."

(Today Bob Montgomery is one of Nashville's top record producers. Sonny Curtis is best known as the writer of such hits as the theme to the Mary Tyler Moore TV show, "I Fought the Law and the Law Won," Leo Sayer's "I Love You More Than I Can Say," and others. He also enjoyed a brief career as a recording artist on Elektra Records.)

Waylon, then about sixteen, was still doing his

show on KVOW in Littlefield. After school he'd travel thirty miles southeast on Highway 84 to Lubbock, to drop in on KDAV and Duncan, whom he knew from the KSEL days.

"We [Waylon and Buddy] were both just startin' out, playin' on a local radio show and doin' a lot of talent contests together [as separate acts], so we got to be friends. . . .

"Buddy was really up, really a good guy. He was really excited about his music, and we never had a cross word. I was his protege, and he did everything he could to help me" (*Photoplay*, February, 1975).

Playing on the "Sunday Dance Party" meant exposure for Waylon and the others, who could then get $10 to $20 playing local parties, movie houses, car lots, and other "venues." On January 5, 1955, Elvis Presley played the Cotton Club in Lubbock in a show sponsored by KDAV. Billed as the "Hillbilly Cat," Presley received $25 for his show.

Inspired by Presley's show, Holly soon formed a more rock-oriented trio, adding Sonny Curtis and Don Guess. Later Holly's group would change members and be called The Crickets.

In early 1958, the Corbin brothers acquired Lubbock radio station KLLL and hired Waylon away from KLVT in nearby Levelland, Texas, where he had been working for a few weeks. Ray "Slim" Corbin was a pleasant character who worked as a DJ and sang in local nightclubs. He gave Jennings the nickname "Waymore." Glenn "Sky" Corbin, more business-oriented than easy-going Slim, managed the station. Brother Larry sold ads and helped keep the books.

They turned it into an all-country station, and added Hi-Pockets Duncan to their staff of air personalities. The station started out with a staff of five.

"Waylon sure didn't have much money at the time," recalled Larry Corbin. "His car didn't work and he couldn't afford to get it fixed, so my father used to drive him from Levelland into Lubbock to work at KLLL every day. Later the station loaned Waylon the money to buy another car.

"I remember Waylon as very shy, a nice guy, and very rural. He didn't dress well at all. He had this old pair of black and white boots that he must have worn every day for a year."

Waylon's starting salary at KLLL was $75 a week. He did two shows a day. At twenty-one, he already had about six years of broadcast experience. He did remotes from fruit-and-vegetable stores and other Lubbock businesses, with Duncan reading the scripts and Waylon singing excerpts from hits of the day.

Hi-Pockets remembered Waylon from the KSEL talent show days. Buddy Holly, when not on the road, spent a good deal of time visiting Hi-Pockets and Waylon at KLLL. They visited either at the studio atop a twenty-story office building, or in the coffee shop one floor below. At one of these coffee sessions Duncan pitched Waylon to Buddy and reintroduced the two. Waylon had been playing Holly's records, and Buddy was grateful. Buddy liked Waylon's voice and decided to help the young singer. He thought Waylon had what it took to be a star.

Buddy was hot then. He had landed a contract with Decca records and was struggling through a disastrous try at recording in Nashville in 1956. The Nashville System that would give Waylon fits in years to come stifled Holly by trying to change his sound. When that didn't work, Buddy hooked up the next year with studio owner/record producer Norman Petty, of Clovis, New Mexico, ninety miles west of Lubbock and just five miles inside the New Mexico border. By then the Crickets included Holly, Jerry Allison, Nikki Sullivan, and Joe B. Mauldin.

Almost immediately Buddy's music caught on, and he scored with hits such as "That'll Be the Day" and "Peggy Sue."

According to Waylon, "Buddy's music was country—with a beat. If he were still living today, I believe he would be considered a country artist. His records aren't any more rock 'n roll than a lot of the country records being made today" (BMI's *Many Worlds of Music*, April 1969).

Waylon soon became one of the most popular DJs at KLLL, which stressed personality radio. He was known for his crazy on-air comments, saying whatever popped into his head, even making occasional boo-boos, which added to his audience appeal. He did a fine job and helped KLLL earn top ratings (it's still the top-rated country station in its market).

Waylon's brother Tommy recalled: "Musicians would gang around K-triple-L. . . . I can close my eyes right now and see Roy [Orbison] leanin' up against a window with them eagle-toed shoes and the sleeves of that white shirt rolled up wishin' that he had a hit record out.

"When Buddy came in, everybody'd look at him like he was God. If he'd a lived, he'd be the greatest country music star. And he would have done it the right way. He was one of the finest men around" (*Roanoke Times & World News*, February 21, 1979).

Holly saw real potential in the singer/DJ Waylon Jennings. After convincing Waylon that he needed to polish his image a bit, he took him to get a haircut and new clothes.

Waylon's financial troubles were in a constant "growth phase"—they were growing worse. Always borrowing money to support himself and his growing family (he and Maxine had two children), he resorted to selling his song "Big Times Ladies Man" to a KLLL co-worker for $20 to satisfy a debt.

Still playing local gigs whenever he could line one up, Waylon got a one-night job sitting in as a bass player in a band backing Ray Price for a show in a nearby town.

Holly eventually arranged for, paid for, produced, and played guitar on Waylon's first record. Waylon's session grew out of a session Holly had already set up for himself with King Curtis, the rhythm-and-blues sax player famous for his work with the Coasters and as a soloist. Buddy paid Curtis's expenses to fly down from New York to Norman Petty's Clovis studio, where Holly and the Crickets had made rock-and-roll history over the previous eighteen months.

Buddy decided to record a single with Waylon at the same October 1958 session. Musicians at Waylon's session included Holly on guitar, Curtis on sax, Tommy Allsup on guitar, George Atwood on bass, and Bo Clarke on drums. Waylon's brother Tommy was there as an observer. (Waylon stayed on after his session to watch Holly record "Reminiscing," which also featured Curtis on sax.)

Waylon's first record was to be "Jole Blon," a Cajun tune with difficult lyrics. It had come to be a popular country dance song, and perhaps Holly and Jennings found appealing the idea of giving it a rockabilly treatment. Buddy and Waylon were familiar with a version recorded by Harry Choates. The first thing they did was sit down and spend a few days trying to decipher the words.

"We sat down and copied the words like we thought they sounded," Waylon said. "A lot of people who heard the results got a lot of laughs out

29

of it. Anyway, we did it with a rock-and-roll beat"
(Grissim).

". . . [A] rhythm & blues saxophonist, a national
rock 'n' roll star, and an aspiring country & western
singer combined forces to record a Cajun waltz with
a west Texas rockabilly beat and lyrics which were
now meaningless in any language" (*The Buddy Holly
Story*, Goldrosen).

The recording was certainly no masterpiece. Waylon's singing is tame and uncertain, and the band
never really sounds together. The other song Waylon
recorded at the October 1958 session was a country
tune written by Lubbock songwriter Bob Vanable,
"When Sin Stops."

Brunswick didn't release "Jole Blon" until March
1959, after Buddy's death. The novel concept in
hybrid musical forms was a commercial flop. "My
first record . . . and my first bomb . . . I hope they
don't find it and re-release it," Waylon said.

In 1972 a private re-issue of Waylon's "Jole Blon"
was made available to collectors in Europe. Also in
1972, a double-album release titled *Good Old Rock
and Roll* was released in Europe, and contained four
early cuts by Waylon, including "When Sin Stops."

According to Maria Holly Santiago, who was married to Buddy for a brief time before he died, Holly
at this stage in his career intended to write for and
produce a number of other artists, including Waylon:
"Like with Waylon Jennings—maybe Buddy thought
Waylon could become a rock 'n' roll star, I don't
know, but he felt sure that Waylon could be popular
in country music, so that's the way he meant to
record him. 'Let's start with something' was his
attitude.

"Buddy meant to be really close to the artists he
chose to work with. He actually wanted Waylon to

come and move in with us — because Buddy felt like that way, he could really come to know Waylon and his feelings, and write songs that matched them" (Goldrosen).

After the October 1958 session Buddy returned to New York, and began discussing with pop tour packager Irving Feld the possibility of taking part in a national concert tour. Feld was the president of Super Enterprises, which packaged the "Biggest Show of Stars," a bill that at various times included Paul Anka, Chuck Berry, Fats Domino, the Everly Brothers, Buddy Knox, and other names of the day. With two other music businessmen, Feld formed General Artists Corporation (GAC) and organized the Winter Dance Party, a three-week tour that would start in mid-January 1959.

Buddy reluctantly agreed to tour as part of the Winter Dance Party. He needed the money, despite the fact that his bank account back in Lubbock contained a sizeable sum (reportedly about $50,000). Norman Petty, Buddy's producer/manager, controlled the account. As he and Holly were then involved in a legal dispute, Petty blocked Buddy's access to the money.

On top of everything else, the original Crickets had decided not to continue with Holly for the time being. Strapped for cash, Buddy decided to form a new Cricket trio for GAC bookings.

Holly returned home to Lubbock for a visit at Christmas 1958. He spent some time with his friends at KLLL, playing some of his new songs for them on guitar and piano.

While Holly was visiting the station one morning, he, Waylon, and Ray "Slim" Corbin decided to write a song. In ten or fifteen minutes it was finished, and someone decided that it should be taped. The tape, less than ninety seconds long, reveals Holly singing and accompanying himself on a borrowed guitar, while Jennings and Corbin try, sometimes unsuccessfully, to match Holly's driving rhythm with handclaps. The song is "You're the One."

"I clapped my hands on that," Waylon said. "Me and Ray Corbin were just standing there. Buddy had most of it written, and he said, 'Help me write this song.' And I don't remember contributing a damn thing! I think the line 'You're the one and I want you to know' is mine. Ray and me were standing there, mostly" (*Guitar Player*, June 1982).

This recording of "You're the One" has since found its way onto various Holly albums.

While he was in Lubbock, Buddy asked Tommy Allsup to play guitar in his group on the Winter Dance tour. Tommy accepted Holly's invitation. Holly then asked Waylon to play bass on the tour. Jennings jumped at the offer, and KLLL reluctantly granted him a leave of absence around Christmas of 1958. Charlie Bunch hired on as a drummer.

Waylon didn't really know how to play the bass guitar. The only other time he had tried was when he had sat as part of the band backing Ray Price. "I was probably the worst rock and roll bass player in the whole world" (*Houston Chronicle*, September 7, 1975).

Jennings studied the bass. He felt a bit intimidated, as he wasn't familiar with the instrument, and he knew Buddy was a perfectionist when it came to music. "I'll tell you what happened. Buddy got me an electric bass and said, 'Look, learn to play this in two weeks.' I think I memorized everything he had ever recorded. Anyway, we'd been out on the road for a couple of weeks, and I suddenly realized that the bass strings are just like the first four strings of a

32

guitar—you know, from the top down—which really amazed me."

Waylon respected Holly's musical instincts and abilities immensely. "I learned a lot of things from him. . .I think he was a *rhythm* player. That doesn't take anything away from his lead playing, but basically the thing that turned him on was rhythm; and that's where he was at. You know, 'Peggy Sue,' the biggest hit he had—the break in it was even rhythm" (*Guitar Player*, June 1982).

Jennings's departure for the tour caused friction between him and Maxine, who was left at home with a two-year-old and a four-month-old. It was another in a continuing series of battles over Waylon's marriage versus his music career. Waylon's career interest won, and he and Allsup drove two hours to the Amarillo airport, then took a flight (Waylon's first) to Wichita. From there they flew to Chicago, and then New York. Waylon says that when he arrived in New York, his neck got stiff from looking at the skyscrapers. He was looking for the Empire State Building—and all the time he was walking around next to it!

Allsup and Jennings stayed with Holly and his new wife Maria at their sparsely-furnished apartment on Fifth Avenue in New York. It was common for Buddy to record songs at home before taking them into the studio to finish; and he, Allsup, and Jennings taped "Peggy Sue Got Married," "That Makes It Tough," "Learning the Game," and other tunes at Holly's apartment while getting ready for the tour. These tracks, in their original form and in overdubbed versions, have appeared on albums released after Holly's death.

"[Buddy] was patient with me, but he was a perfectionist. He had things down to a detail on the things that he played. Like on those tapes that he did in his apartment — just little things — you can hear how much he put into it. I was learning as I went along. We could've been better, given time, but I had to be driving him nuts. As far as being critical, I think he was harder on himself than anybody else" (*Guitar Player*, June 1982).

The tour began the third week of January 1959 as Buddy's single, "It Doesn't Matter Any More," was climbing the pop charts.

The "Winter Dance Party" was a tour through the heart of the Midwest at the coldest time of the year, with most of the appearances scheduled in Minnesota, Wisconsin, and Iowa. This leg of the Winter Dance Party had just five acts: Holly, Ritchie Valens ("Donna," "La Bamba"), J. P. "The Big Bopper" Richardson ("Chantilly Lace"), Dion and the Belmonts ("Runaround Sue"), and newcomer Frankie Sardo.

The tour started on January 23 in Milwaukee, where it was twenty-five degrees below zero. Waylon and the rest of the band were nattily attired on stage in black sports coats, light colored shirts with yellow ascots, and grey trousers. Not long into the tour one band member lost his stage clothes, so the group had to resort to brown pants and checkered sports coats, their only other matching outfits. Buddy still wore the black and grey outfit.

". . . Buddy was a hillbilly. We sat on buses singin' Hank Williams songs with Dion. And 'Salty Dog Blues,' we did that song on stage and people thought it was rock 'n roll" (*Houston Chronicle*, September 7, 1975). The new Crickets opened Holly's set, Buddy joined Waylon in singing "Salty Dog Blues," then

Holly and the group served up energetic versions of Buddy's hits.

Waylon and fellow Texan Richardson (he came from Beaumont) became friends. On the bus they wrote a song intended for George Jones, "Move Over Blues," though the song has since been lost, and Waylon can't remember the words.

Dion, who was nineteen when he was on the Winter Dance tour, recalled that as bad as things were, they enjoyed the miserable tour conditions in a way. "It was sub-zero weather and the bus kept breaking down. But we all got along together just great. . . . We were young kids . . . you think you can walk through walls then, and you don't realize how dangerous it can be," he said. "That tour, despite all its problems, was a field day for sharing songs and experiences" (*Boston Herald American*, July 31, 1978).

The rickety converted school bus that GAC provided for the tour froze up somewhere between Duluth, Minnesota, and Green Bay, Wisconsin, on January 31. Charlie Bunch suffered frostbite on his feet as a result of being stranded in the cold, and Dion replaced him on drums during Holly's sets.

Traveling on this bus under any condition would not have been comfortable, but in this extreme cold it was downright hazardous. The group left each town after the show was over, at midnight or later, and traveled in the freezing darkness, three hundred to six hundred miles to the next date. They had to switch buses several times during the early part of the tour, as mechanical problems sidelined the vehicles. They'd pull into the new town around mid-day to try to catch some sleep before it was time to get ready for that night's show.

On February 1 the group played afternoon and

evening concerts in Appleton and Green Bay, Wisconsin. Green Bay went well and the Dance Party piled into the bus for the three-hundred-and-fifty-mile trip to Clear Lake, ten miles west of Mason City in north central Iowa. After still more bus trouble the group finally pulled into Clear Lake at 6 p.m. on February 2. They had no time to rest — the show was scheduled to start at 8 p.m.

The dance was to last until midnight. Immediately afterward, the performers were to climb back onto the bus and ride all night four hundred and thirty miles northwest to Moorhead, Minnesota, where they were booked for two shows the night of February 3.

On arriving in Clear Lake, Holly was as exhausted as the rest of the performers. "We hadn't been in a hotel for six or seven days," Waylon said. "Our clothes were all dirty and we were tired . . ." (*Music City News*, May 1966). At Clear Lake, Buddy decided to charter a small plane to carry him and his sidemen to Fargo, North Dakota, where they would catch a commercial flight to Moorhead. Buddy figured this arrangement would allow them to get a decent sleep and the chance to get the laundry done before the next night's shows.

Holly explained his plan to Jennings and Allsup, and all agreed to split the $108 cost of renting the plane three ways. The pilot who owned the local flying service was away on another job, so his twenty-one year old assistant, Roger Peterson, said he would fly the three musicians to Fargo.

When Valens and Richardson heard about the flight arrangement, they decided it sounded like a good idea. Valens asked Allsup if he'd give up his seat, and Richardson, who had been suffering from the flu for days, approached Waylon backstage at Clear Lake and asked about taking his place on the plane.

Waylon, like Dion, didn't mind the uncomfortable tour conditions as much as the more experienced road acts; for him the tour was a novelty. He agreed to let Richardson make the flight in his place, and Allsup did the same for Valens.

Between 1,100 and 1,500 teenagers packed the Surf Ballroom to see the Dance Party that night. When the Clear Lake show was over, the Surf's manager drove Holly, Richardson, and Valens to the Mason City Airport, where they were met by Roger Peterson. Peterson was not aware of special weather advisories that might have changed his mind about flying. The advisories warned of snow and fog in the area that the young pilot would be flying through. These conditions would require instrument flying, for which Peterson was not certified.

About 1 a.m. the single-engine four-seater took off from Clear Lake. It will never be known for certain what happened. They probably encountered snow and winds, causing Peterson, because of stress and inexperience, to lose control of the plane, which crashed in a cornfield about eight miles from the airport. All four passengers were killed on impact.

The tragic loss of Holly's talent (not to mention that of Valens and Richardson), has been immortalized in Don McLean's "American Pie" as "the day the music died."

The wreckage wasn't discovered until 9:30 the morning of February 3. Shortly after noon Holly's sidemen and the other Dance Party performers pulled into Moorhead. Tommy got off the bus and walked into the hotel. As he passed through the lobby, he saw a photograph of J. P. Richardson on the screen of a nearby television, but the sound was turned down and he couldn't tell what the announcer was saying. The desk clerk filled Allsup in on what had happened.

Early news accounts of the accident reported that Allsup and Jennings were also killed in the crash, though Tommy and Waylon weren't aware of this at the time. The confusion stemmed in part from the fact that Allsup's wallet had been found near the plane. Tommy had given it to Buddy so that Buddy could pick up a registered letter for him in Moorhead. In addition, Waylon's name was on the back of a card in Allsup's wallet, and of course it was known that Allsup and Jennings were Holly's sidemen on the tour. A Mason City radio station put out the news that Holly and Allsup had been on the plane. It was assumed that Holly's musician friends from Lubbock had also been killed.

Waylon felt numb. He'd been asleep all night on the bus, and when he woke up the first thing he heard was that Holly and the other stars of the tour were dead. He walked around in a daze. "I didn't know what to do. I was shocked. I just stood around for an hour not knowing what to do . . .

"It just seemed like such a waste of lives. I felt responsible, like God had cheated somebody. I was pretty young, and it took me a while to get back on the right track" (*Music City News*, May 1966). Waylon couldn't bring himself to look at police photos of the crash until almost 15 years later. To this day he is deeply affected by Holly's death.

After a while Waylon pulled himself together enough to phone home to Lubbock. He learned that for the past three hours Maxine and his mother had believed that he was dead. "In West Texas at that time of the year, they had bad weather and trouble with the teletype machines. All they had got out of the machine was Buddy Holly, then some garbled names which they couldn't make out, then Buddy Holly and his band.

"As you can imagine, they were all in pretty bad shape when I called. The radio stations had announced it [their deaths], so they really had no other information to go by" (*Photoplay*, February, 1975).

In Moorhead, the surviving performers at first didn't want to go through with their engagement. They wanted to quit the tour and accompany Buddy's body back to Lubbock. GAC and the booking agents promised them a paid flight to Buddy's funeral if they continued with the tour. They also promised to continue to pay the group the same money for the remaining sixteen shows. This would have amounted to about $4,000 for the group for the two weeks (Waylon earned around $200 a week at the time). Allsup and Jennings really needed the money, so with the understanding that they would be able to attend Buddy's funeral, they agreed to go on with the show.

The concerts after Holly's death were emotionally draining for the performers and audience alike. When Holly's group appeared on stage minus its star and sang Buddy's songs, there was hardly a dry eye in the house.

After getting the new Crickets to carry on, GAC quickly changed its tune about the money. "[GAC] tried to dock us for the money Holly, Valens, and the Bopper would have gotten — this after begging us to play. We just wanted to go home, but we played anyway. Real nice people, them . . . ," Waylon said (*Boston Herald American*, July 31, 1978).

On February 4 a plane was sent from Lubbock to bring Buddy's body home, but the storm system had moved into Iowa, and it was February 5 before the plane could return to Texas with Holly's remains. Services were held in Lubbock on February 7.

GAC didn't fly the Winter Dance Crickets to the funeral as they had promised. The group played Des Moines the day Buddy was buried. Springfield, Illinois, was the final stop on the tour, February 15, 1959. Allsup, Jennings, and the others boarded their bus for the last time, and rode it to Chicago, where they caught a train to New York.

On the way home Waylon had been ribbing a couple of the other guys on the tour about popping little white pills. Two of the performers supposedly retaliated by slipping some pills into Waylon's drink, and Jennings stayed awake over the next three days while they made their way to New York.

In New York Waylon and the others intended to settle with GAC. They were disgusted to find that GAC intended to keep none of the verbal promises they had made following Buddy's death.

Coincidentally, the original Crickets were in New York with Petty at the same time, suing over use of the band's name. An agreement was reached whereby GAC would continue with Crickets Joe B. Mauldin, Jerry Allison, Allsup, and Earl Sinks. Waylon, Sonny Curtis (who had come up with Petty and the others), and two others would return to Texas.

Waylon has always been careful to point out that he was not a true Cricket. "When Buddy was alive, it was J. I. [Allison], and Joe B. [Mauldin] who were the Crickets, period. On that last tour, me, Tommy Allsup, and Carl Bunch were just backing Buddy up. Nobody could take the place of the Crickets" (*Guitar Player*, June 1982). For legal reasons and out of friendship to the original Crickets, Holly probably did not refer to his backup group on the Winter Dance Party as the Crickets.

"A lot of people have written that I was an original Cricket, but that's not true, y'know? I never was really a Cricket. Buddy and the Crickets decided to got their own ways for a while at one point. They were gonna get back together again, which they never did, of course.

"I was Buddy's protege. That's what it basically amounted to. He needed a bass player and I worked in a band. . . . He was my friend. That was the main thing in our relationship. He got me started and was the first guy to ever have faith in me as a singer" (*The Aquarian*, February 24–March 3, 1982).

Demoralized and disillusioned after Buddy's death, Waylon decided to give up road work and a solo career. He had no thoughts of playing on stage again.

It was at this point that Sonny, Waylon, and the two others drove back to Lubbock in a new 1958 Chevrolet that Jerry Allison let them use. The engine burned out in Missouri.

That's about how Waylon felt, too.

Chapter Four

After the Music Died

If February 3, 1959, was the day the music died for rock fans, it was the day the future died for Waylon. He could see his hopes and dreams fading. He went back to Lubbock and quit singing.

With Buddy gone, there didn't seem to be much point in pursuing a music career. Waylon's association with Holly, however brief, was to have a lasting effect on his music. He wrote and recorded a song called "Stars in Heaven," a tribute to Buddy Holly, The Big Bopper, Ritchie Valens, and other stars of the same era who had died young. A later Jennings-written song, "Just To Satisfy You," had a certain amount of Holly influence as well.

"Buddy was just great," Waylon said in a televised interview with WSMV-Nashville's Dan Miller. "He was up all the time, happy. He loved music, by golly. At that time, he had ideas that were really way ahead. He was the first to come along after Elvis with his own thing, a white rock 'n roll singer" (Nashville *Tennessean*, July 9, 1983).

In May 1973 and May 1974 Waylon went into the studio with several members of the original Crickets to cut material.

Waylon has recorded these tributes to Holly: "The Stage," "Old Friend" (on 1976's *Are Your Ready for the Country*), plus a medley of Buddy Holly hits on 1978's *I've Always Been Crazy*. Waylon had intended to record an entire album of Holly songs, but when he looked closely at the lyrics he decided they were too dated.

"[Holly] was a rhythm guitar picker, and that's basically what I am. He taught me that you can take country songs and put different rhythms to 'em. He taught me calypso-type things, and 'straight-A' things like 'Peggy Sue,' and things like taking a waltz and doin' it in $6/8$ time instead of the usual $3/4$.

"But mainly, what I learned from Buddy was an attitude. He loved music, and he taught me that it shouldn't have any barriers to it."

Years later, when Waylon was an established night-club act in Phoenix, Holly was still often on his mind: "After Buddy died, we were playing at a club in Phoenix called J.D.'s and we were like the hottest thing there, a good crowd every night and standing room only on the weekends.

"So, one night I said to Richie [Albright (Waylon's drummer for many years)], 'Well, I think it's time to leave.' And Richie said, 'Leave? With this kind of crowd really digging what we're doing?'

"I said, 'Yep. That's one thing I learned from Buddy. If you leave now, when you're ahead, they'll exaggerate how good it was. But if you wait till it's all over, when you're starting to lose it, they'll exaggerate how bad it was' " (*Guitar Player*, June 1982).

Waylon believes Buddy was the only one to come out of the Elvis era with "his own thing. It never came back until the Beatles." He says you can hear Holly all over the Beatles' sound (even the Beatles' name was a takeoff of Holly's Crickets).

"Something else—[Buddy] was great on stage. Besides that, he was really a great person. He had a personal magnetism which very few people have. When he came on stage he'd get applause because he was Buddy Holly, but it wasn't long before he had the house completely captured. He didn't jump around too much . . . there was excitement in his singing . . . he knew how to communicate from the stage to the people."

The Buddy Holly Story, a financially successful and critically acclaimed feature film based on Holly's life (with numerous embellishments), opened in theaters across America in August 1978. Waylon didn't appear in the movie and was not represented in it. He had these comments on the film: "A lot of it wasn't true. All in all, though, I think it's a great movie. The casting director was great. I was too old for a part, though. I think Gary Busey did a great job, except I do think he could have learned the songs" (*Minneapolis Star*, July 24, 1978).

Oddly, a few months later Waylon voiced an entirely different opinion: "Oh, I hated it! It was a bunch of baloney! I didn't like any of it. The killer is that the *real* story would have been so much better— they didn't have to juice up his story" (*Houston Post*, January 19, 1979).

In any event, Waylon is today what Buddy envisioned he would be—a giant among country music performers.

In mid-February 1959 when Waylon returned to Lubbock from New York, he was bitterly disappointed and heartsick at the loss of Buddy Holly. He had also gotten his first lesson on how the music industry could play Screw The Artist.

44

"We finished that tour and then I quit playing music for about a year after that. I took my guitar over to my mother's and put it in the back room.

"It affected me in a lot of ways. I became irresponsible as far as my work was concerned. I was completely mixed up. I couldn't have cared less about being a disc jockey. Everything got progressively worse. I quit jobs when I really shouldn't have and wound up working as a mechanic's helper" (*Music City News*, May 1966).

Waylon was bitter toward Norman Petty for his treatment of Holly and his control over the artist's finances and music. He took jabs at Petty for taking partial credit on songs that Waylon said were all Holly's, for example, "Peggy Sue": "Norman [Petty] probably changed one word, which one I don't know, but I know of some times where he's been known to take part of a song, which is ridiculous" (*Popular Music & Society*, No. 3, 1974).

In his depressed state of mind, Waylon even felt that Petty was in part responsible for Holly's death, as Buddy had been forced to go on the Winter Dance Party tour because he was so short of cash.

Twenty-two-year-old Jennings, getting his first taste of the seamy side of the music business, had earlier watched with disbelief as Holly's label, Brunswick, squabbled with its own parent company, Decca, over the rights to Holly's masters. Decca had originally recorded Holly in 1956 in Nashville, and initially threatened to prevent release of Buddy's music when it learned that Brunswick had signed him. "A company suing itself—that seemed pretty strange at the time," Waylon said.

All this, compounded by the Crickets' temporary parting of ways with Holly, and GAC's broken promises and crass treatment of its road acts, left a bad taste in Waylon's mouth.

Brunswick released Waylon's "Jole Blon" in March 1959, one month after Buddy's death. One wonders whether Brunswick was only releasing the record to capitalize on Holly's death. The single was a dud, adding to Waylon's depression, though he was already tucking away his music dreams.

In Lubbock, the Corbins gladly took Waylon back at his $75-a-week job as a DJ at KLLL. "After he came back from the Holly tour, Waylon was accustomed to making more money than he used to at the station," said Larry Corbin, who headed ad sales at KLLL. "He told me he'd have to find a way to make more money. So I was going to teach him to sell spots [ads], and he'd get a commission on the sales.

"I'd take him around with me when I called on customers, so he could watch me deliver the sales pitch. Then, after a while, I took him in to a customer, and Waylon was going to deliver the pitch himself.

"But when we got inside and it was time to give the pitch he elbowed me and whispered, 'Go ahead, I can't do it.' As a salesman Waylon was an utter failure!"

Also working at KLLL was Don Bowman, a funny, wild-spirited DJ who joined the station in March 1959, right after Waylon returned from the Holly tour. He was destined to become one of Waylon's best friends. Jennings and Bowman made commercials and even collected station bills in addition to handling their on-air duties.

Legend has it that when Bowman and Jennings got bored at KLLL, they'd cue up a Navy recruiting disc, which was a forty-five minute pre-packaged show complete with music and fillers, and then go downstairs to the bowling alley in the same building. One

46

time Sky caught them and erected a sign in the studio:

DON BOWMAN AND WAYLON JENNINGS NOT TO BE
IN THE CONTROL ROOM AT THE SAME TIME
WHILE ON THE AIR.

Being a DJ wasn't fulfilling for Waylon any more. He took a more casual attitude toward his on-air work, at times testing the limits of the FCC code. He tried some other jobs, too. "[Around 1960] I worked as a mechanic's helper and drove a school bus, which was my only source of income, and then I woke up! I decided that wasn't getting it, so I started back to disc jockeying . . .

"Then I formed a band and started working night clubs. I worked the road for a while, but I found out you don't do this if you don't know who you are" (*Music City News*, May 1966).

Waylon and his band played clubs in a wide area out from Lubbock. He knew that this was the way he wanted to go, that writing, recording, and singing music was what he wanted to do for a living. He also knew he couldn't accomplish that in Lubbock.

Waylon's final job in Texas was working a few weeks at KDAV before moving himself and his family to Phoenix, where he intended to "make it" in the music business, or die trying.

Chapter Five

Phoenix: Live at J.D.'s

In 1961, while Chubby Checker was urging us to twist and the Tokens were chanting "The Lion Sleeps Tonight," Waylon Jennings packed up his family and moved from Lubbock about six hundred miles due west to Phoenix. In short order he worked part-time as a DJ, played guitar and sang in local nightclubs, and put together a sound that would change country music forever.

Waylon's move was made under pressure — he had to find a way to make more money, and he had to find a way to make his mark as a singer. His credit in Lubbock was not exactly the best, and he had a new addition to the family to support: Buddy Dean, born March 21, 1961. The name Buddy stood for Holly, and Dean was after 1950s film star James Dean. In the midst of all this, Waylon's marriage to Maxine was slowly coming apart at the seams. She resented more than ever Waylon's need to launch a career as a performer, and she feared losing him if he became a star.

Waylon was deeply affected by his stay in Phoenix: "That's where I more or less developed everything — my way of thinking." Socially and musically, Phoenix in those days was something like a blend of Los Angeles, Nashville, and Texas. Waylon's audience included oil barons, cowboys, longhairs, migrant workers, the blue-collar factory crowd, Chicanos, tourists, and all sorts of others. The clubs Waylon played drew folks from downtown Phoenix plus such suburbs as Mesa, Sun City, Glendale, Tempe, and Scottsdale, as well as from cities several hours' drive away.

Actually Waylon's first move was to Coolidge, Arizona, about forty miles southeast of Phoenix, where he landed a job as an afternoon DJ on KCKY. "Maxine's sister lived there at the time," Tommy Jennings recalled. "Waylon and Maxine had visited there in the late '50s."

Waylon worked days at KCKY and sang nights at several local nightclubs, including the Sage and Sand and the Goose.

Waylon next moved to Phoenix, where in three years of playing six nights a week he became one of the hottest acts in the Southwest, eventually making his way up to playing J.D.'s, one of the hottest clubs in several states.

According to Frankie Shadid, who owned a Phoenix club called Frankie's back in those days, Waylon looked for work in clubs all around Phoenix before getting his first job, at Wild Bill's—but his stay there ended after only three weeks when he got into a row with Wild Bill himself. Waylon played a club in Coolidge for the next few weeks, then switched to Frankie's from January through May of 1962. Frankie's seated only about 75 people, and initially Waylon says he drew "about five people on Friday and five more on Saturday."

"It was real tough in 1962 in Phoenix," Frankie said (*Phoenix Gazette*, August 5, 1980). "There was a construction strike and there wasn't any real growth. All the places did poor."

Around May of 1962 Waylon decided to try his luck up north, so he put together a road band to play jobs in Idaho, Montana, and Utah. (Utah's border is about two hundred and thirty miles north of Phoenix.) The tour was cut short when the band broke up in Salt Lake City. It was probably on this tour that Jennings met Utah native Lynne Gladys Jones, who would soon become his second wife.

One month later Waylon was back on Frankie's doorstep. "I told him, 'Waylon, I can't afford you,' " Frankie said. "So he went all over Phoenix looking for a job and couldn't find one. Finally, I hired him back." Frankie paid Waylon $120 a week, his rhythm guitarist $60, and his bass player $20." Waylon's bass player only played weekends—and Waylon had no drummer.

Things soon got better for Shadid and Jennings, as Waylon and his group packed the house to over-full, about a hundred people almost every night.

Now called Waylon Jennings and the Waylors, the act was building a strong local following. Before the end of 1962 Waylon's marriage to Maxine ended in divorce, and Waylon, twenty-five, married for a second time. On December 12, 1962, he drove two hundred and seventy miles northwest to Las Vegas to marry Lynne, employed at the time as a waitress at Wild Bill's, where she drew attention as a barmaid with her salty language. Waylon's guitar player Jerry Gropp witnessed the ceremony.

As with his first wife, Waylon married Lynne thinking she was pregnant. She was, but shortly after the couple returned from Las Vegas and rented an apartment in Scottsdale she miscarried. Lynne was never in the best of health during her marriage to

Waylon. The couple later adopted a baby girl, Tomi, born January 17, 1964.

On rare slow nights Jennings left Frankie's early (and received only half a night's pay) to pick Lynne up at Wild Bill's. "The kid [Waylon] worked hard," Shadid said. "He would play two, three hours straight without a break. As long as there was someone in the audience, he played. The band would take breaks, but not Waylon."

In those days Waylon played "commercial" songs such as "Cotton Fields" and "Jambalaya," music guaranteed to make the dance floor shake and keep the bar glasses hopping. Largely because of Waylon's popularity, Frankie's expanded from a 75-seat club to a 150-seater.

Frankie and Waylon never had a written contract—each trusted the other's word. As business got better, Frankie raised Waylon's pay. By late 1962 Frankie was paying the band $600 a week, half of which went to Waylon. "Every time Waylon would come up to me and say that some other place was making him an offer, I gave him a raise," Frankie said.

In 1963 Waylon found yet another job as DJ, this time as an afternoon air personality at KHAT. Many country artists Waylon would later become associated with—including Bobby Barc and Tompall and the Glaser Brothers—would recall first meeting Waylon at KHAT.

In August 1963 Waylon left Frankie's for the Cross Keys club and another stint at Wild Bill's. A cleanup man Waylon knew at Wild Bill's in the early 1960s was skilled in working with leather, and he made the hand-tooled leather piece that still adorns Waylon's 1963 Telecaster guitar. Jennings also worked the Bird Cage in Scottsdale, and Matt's in Prescott, about seventy miles northeast of Phoenix. At Matt's, in

1964, he met and hired a young drummer named Richie Albright. Over the next two decades Jerry Gropp and Albright would remain Waylon's band members and best friends.

With the addition of drummer Richie Albright to his band in 1964, Waylon began to crystallize the bottom-heavy, pulsating, at times rock-inspired beat that is now his trademark.

"We also played a place called Mr. Magoo's around that time," said Tommy Jennings, who moved to Phoenix from Littlefield to play bass in Waylon's band in 1965. Magoo's in Tempe was owned by two men (Richard Guimont and James David Musil, Sr.) who would later be partners in J.D.'s nightclub in Phoenix.

Waylon's big break came when he was hired in July 1964 to play the newly-built J.D.'s. He played the large country room upstairs (it seated 600) — downstairs was a rock room. He also began recording, and gaining the attention of visiting music industry figures. ". . . [F]riends of mine were building a new club called J.D.'s, and before they started construction we made a deal whereby I would play there," Waylon said. "I even helped them with part of the design work and things like that. After the place opened I ended up working there for about eighteen months.

". . . [T]he cross-section that we drew was unbelievable . . . we drew the college students, doctors, lawyers, and *all* the cowboys. . . . We were predominantly country and yet what I started doing was to take pop tunes or tunes that I felt that I could relate to as a . . . country person" (Grissim).

J.D.'s became a "happening" nightspot in the Southwest in the 1960s. Waylon found his musical style amid the clash of various cultures under J.D.'s roof. He gave country, rock, and folk tunes his own interpretation, always with special attention to a heavy, moving beat and straight-from-the-heart lyrics. When he performed a slow song you could hear a pin drop, and when he sang a fast song you could feel the walls shake. When Waylon found music that moved young and old, straight and "hippy," cowboys and accountants, he knew he was on to something big.

Waylon also found time to do some radio jingle work, at one point creating Waylon's Hit Parade, a series of drive-in theater intermission tapes that featured Waylon's smooth intros and snack bar suggestions.

In Phoenix in 1962 Waylon hooked up with Audio Recorders, an organization that had its own record label, Ramco. Waylon had recorded his Trend Records sides at Audio Recorders. (Floyd Ramsey, president of Ramco, leased the recordings Waylon had made earlier for Trend Records.) This outlet gave Jennings valuable studio experience as a musician, arranger, singer, and producer, as Ramco was a fairly active label.

Trend '61 (the label changed names with each year) had released their first Waylon Jennings single in 1961: "Another Blue Day"/"Never Again," which listed Wendell Bagwell as Waylon's producer/manager. Trend '63 released "My Baby Walks All Over Me"/"The Stage" in 1963. "The Stage" was Waylon's tribute to Buddy Holly and several other rock stars who had met early deaths, including Eddie Cochran, Ritchie Valens, and The Big Bopper.

(Floyd Ramsey's Ramco Records re-released these songs—except "The Stage"—in 1967, after Waylon had two years of popularity as an RCA artist. Waylon destroyed the masters to "The Stage", originally titled "Stars in Heaven," because he was not happy with the sound of the recording. Ramsey substituted "My World" for "The Stage" in his 1967 release.)

Waylon's KLLL-Lubbock buddy, Don Bowman, had stayed in radio work full time, and by 1963 was working at KDEL in San Diego, California. Bowman got some free airline coupons from a friend, and began flying into Phoenix every two or three weeks to write songs with Waylon. They holed up in Bowman's Phoenix motel room (Lynne had a hard time believing Waylon was away from home so often just "writing songs") and in marathon sessions lasting up to eighteen hours proceeded to collaborate on about twenty songs, two of which are "Anita, You're Dreaming" and "Just to Satisfy You."

Bowman and Jennings, both sharp-witted and given to healthy sarcasm, were amazed at how often a line they jokingly tossed out turned out to fit perfectly into one of their serious, sad songs. Not all their tunes were serious—they took a thinly veiled swipe at Lynne with "Poor Ole Ugly Gladys Jones."

By 1963 Bowman was pitching songs by mail from San Diego to Chet Atkins, RCA-Nashville's top executive and best record producer. (Chet eventually produced some comedy records by Bowman.) Bowman also developed a good rapport with Jerry Moss, co-owner of the fledgling independent label Carnival Records, soon to be renamed A&M, and whose main artist was Moss's trumpet-playing partner, Herb Alpert. Bowman gave Moss Waylon's recordings of "Just to Satisfy You" and "Four Strong Winds," as well as Waylon's Trend Records tracks.

Moss was lukewarm about Waylon's recordings, mainly because of their inferior studio quality. Herb was knocked out by Waylon's voice. He sensed that he was listening to a potential star, and felt he could

54

capture and polish that quality for A&M.

In April 1964, A&M signed Waylon to three-year recording and publishing agreements (publishing was with A&M's Irving Music subsidiary), and immediately issued a single, "Love Denied"/"Rave On"—which didn't even receive enough airplay to register on *Billboard* magazine's country singles chart.

Herb cut a total of fourteen tracks on Waylon, recording sometimes in Phoenix, sometimes in Hollywood, and sometimes taking Phoenix tracks and overdubbing them in Hollywood. A&M issued three more singles in 1964–65, none of which charted: "Four Strong Winds"/"Just to Satisfy You," "Sing the Girls a Song, Bill"/"The Race Is On" and "I Don't Believe You"/"The Real House of the Rising Sun."

Alpert and Moss were—and still are—extremely creative and innovative in recording and marketing music for the popular market. But in 1964 it became apparent that A&M lacked the marketing and promotional expertise to do business in the specialized country market. Waylon was growing extremely frustrated with his A&M situation. He liked Alpert, but was shocked to hear how his tracks came out sounding after Herb "sweetened them" in Hollywood. It became clear that Alpert and Waylon had entirely different ideas about how Waylon should sound.

For example, Waylon's "Sing the Girls a Song, Bill" on A&M is a folk-music-like singalong, while his "Rave On" chugs along like a midtempo 1960s rocker until the Tijuana Brass are plunked into the middle of it. Waylon knew something wasn't right, and he resisted Alpert's tinkering with the sound whenever possible. He admits that he "probably put a few gray hairs" in Alpert's head.

"Herb was a good friend, but he wouldn't let me

record my own songs. And we really couldn't communicate in a recording studio. He wanted something out of me that I didn't know about. . . . Except since then, I figured out that he heard an Al Martino in me that just wasn't there."

Waylon finally concluded that Herb didn't really like country music, "but then he didn't consider me a country singer. I thought I was a country singer—really. But now I'm just a singer." If that sounds confusing, that's because it is. Neither Jennings nor Alpert knew exactly how to capture the Jennings sound on record in 1964. Teaming Jennings and A&M was the wrong idea at the wrong time. A&M has wisely steered clear of country marketing since those days, with the exception of an occasional single release.

The A&M period was one of experimentation for Waylon and Alpert, though neither saw it as such at the time. Alpert heard a potential for a certain slickness in Waylon's voice that he was trying to bring out by overdubbing elements and sounds which were foreign to the basic tracks Waylon cut.

Waylon's lack of direction was reflected in his scattered song selection. He'd try a bit of Holly's rockabilly sound ("Rave On"), go hard-core country with George Jones's "The Race Is On," then reach outside the traditional country sphere for a folk tune ("Four Strong Winds") and sample the folk scene with Bob Dylan's "Don't Think Twice."

During this period, Bowman, RCA artist Bobby Bare, and Nashville songwriter/publisher Harlan Howard were lobbying Chet Atkins to sign Waylon. When Chet eventually called Waylon in late 1964, Jennings jumped at the offer—he knew he was a country artist, not a pop artist, and he knew his chances of succeeding in the country market were infinitely better with the names RCA and Chet Atkins behind him. Waylon accepted Chet's offer, but then had to convince Alpert and Moss to release him from his contracts.

Moss admitted that A&M couldn't further Waylon's career and thought they should release him. Herb stuck by his guns. He didn't want to let Waylon go, and according to Waylon "offered me (four or five percent) of A&M to stay with him. I hate to count how much money I'd be worth today [if I'd taken the offer]. Quite a bit!"

A&M finally gave Waylon his release in 1965, though they held him to his Irving Music contract, which wouldn't expire until April of 1967. In theory this meant that Irving Music would own the publishing rights to the songs Waylon would write over the next two years. Alpert and Moss saw this as a way for A&M to recoup its investment in Waylon, in the event that his songs became successful on RCA.

A&M didn't release an album on Jennings until 1970, but the freshness of that release (*Don't Think Twice*) six years after the songs were cut shows how Waylon's country sound of the mid-1960s was ahead of its time.

While Waylon was "between contracts" he recorded *Waylon Jennings at J.D.'s*, a promotional album on Sound Records that could only be obtained through the nightclub. Though many assume it is a live album cut at the club, it was in fact recorded at Audio Recorders for less than $100, which was paid by J.D.'s owner James David (J.D.) Music, Sr. It included Waylon's version of Buddy Holly's "It's So Easy." Decca Records later obtained the masters to this album and released them in mid-1969 as an album titled *Waylon Jennings*. Copies of the J.D.'s album have reportedly sold for hundreds of dollars to collectors.

Waylon also made a number of appearances on a Saturday afternoon show on KHAT-TV, which was owned by the same man who owned KHAT radio. Waylon produced and sang or played guitar on a number of projects at Audio Recorders, and a lot of his work found its way out on releases. He played lead guitar on *Cowboy's Sweetheart*, a Patsy Montana album released on Starday, and co-wrote and recorded "My World," which replaced "The Stage" in Ramco's 1967 reissues of his material. The year 1965 also brought the bootleg release of Jennings covers of Roy Orbison songs on Bat Records: "Crying"/ "Dream Baby."

How did Waylon juggle his day work at KHAT, his night work in clubs, his songwriting sessions with Bowman, and his other recording and promotional efforts? Easy. As far back as 1963, he'd found that those little pills that had kept him awake at the end of the Buddy Holly tour in 1959 really came in useful when he needed to play late into the night, or to stay up for eighteen hours writing songs. In Phoenix, Waylon developed an addiction to amphetamines which would lead to a life-threatening cocaine addiction. His drug use for the next three decades would be the most serious obstacle between him and happiness, let alone professional stability (more on this in Chapter 11).

Around 1964 Waylon met another struggling music figure who would make his own mark on country music history: Willie Nelson. Waylon asked Willie's advice on Chet's offer to sign with RCA. Willie, who had recently signed with RCA himself, and who was already experiencing some of the pains that Waylon would later endure, advised against making the move.

58

"We were instant friends," Willie recalled. "He asked me for some friendly advice on moving to Nashville, giving up a good job with a higher than average income (at J.D.'s) to dig for some gold on Nashville's 16th Avenue concrete. Naturally, I told him to stay where he was. Fortunately, he didn't listen" (*Country Style*, 1978).

Another person who opposed Waylon's desire to move to Nashville was his wife, Lynne. In poor health (she had kidney trouble, among other ailments) and skeptical of Waylon's chances of making it in the record business, Lynne hated the idea of Waylon accepting RCA's offer. She was equally insecure about holding on to Waylon in the event that he did become successful on RCA. Their marriage was already on the rocks, and she was sure this would prove to be one of the last reasons for it falling apart.

Ironically, the same two songs that had attracted A&M to Waylon—"Four Strong Winds" and "Just to Satisfy You"—led to Jennings being signed by RCA. The latter, which had failed as an A&M Jennings release, was covered for a number-three country smash by Bobby Bare in late 1964. Bobby went to number thirty-one in late 1965 with Waylon's composition "Just to Satisfy You."

These successes, combined with Waylon's talent— and the urgings of Bare, Bowman, and songwriter/ publisher Harlan Howard—brought Waylon to the attention of Bare's producer, Chet Atkins.

Bobby Bare, then a hot RCA artist, had first heard about Waylon from Don Bowman during a visit to KDEL in 1964. He experienced Jennings's magic for himself when he dropped in at Waylon's show at J.D.'s in 1964–65. "Chet, you gotta sign that ole boy up," Bare recalled saying. "He's one of the best I've heard in ages. . . . I know I'm cuttin' my own throat by doin' it, because he's doing the same thing I'm doing . . . but he deserves to be on a major label" (*Waylon & Willie*, Allen).

Bowman continued to pepper Atkins with suggestions about recording Waylon's songs or, better yet, signing the artist himself. Howard, who co-published both Bare's and Bowman's songs, liked Waylon's music and had a vested interest in promoting the artist.

The pressure tactics eventually worked, and shortly before Christmas of 1964 Waylon got a phone call from Chet asking him to consider signing with RCA. Waylon signed with RCA and began recording for the label in Nashville that spring.

He thought his troubles were over—but they were just beginning.

Chapter Six

Nashville: "Are You Sure Hank Done It This Way?"

In early 1965 Waylon Jennings, then twenty-eight, signed with RCA Records and recorded his first tracks for the label.

Waylon moved to Nashville seven years after Buddy Holly's death, as something Holly always knew he could be — a major label artist. Ironically, he encountered the same obstacle that had temporarily stalled Holly's career in 1956: a Nashville music system that insisted on changing his sound.

Waylon left Phoenix in 1965 with something he didn't have when he had arrived in that city around 1961: a unique musical style. The plodding, heavy rhythms, intimate coordination of Waylon and his band, and extra flavor that Waylon's own guitar playing added were all elements important to his new sound. They were also elements that didn't fit into the smooth musical assembly line that Nashville operated at the time.

Music Row, in 1965, was just a few buildings on 16th and 17th Avenues South in Nashville, but it housed publishing and record label executives who had a stranglehold on the country music sound of their day.

Waylon came to Nashville naive about the politics behind Nashville's music industry, and about then-current Nashville recording techniques. For example, the session players enjoyed a quiet laugh when the tape started to roll at Waylon's first RCA session, and Jennings stepped up to the microphone ready to sing and play guitar at the same time. He didn't realize that producers usually added guitar leads on later overdub sessions.

Waylon expected to use his Waylors in the studio, and he wanted to cut songs that had been written and recorded by pop, folk, and rock writers. In short, he did everything that country recording artists weren't "supposed" to do in the mid-1960s.

In fairness, the Nashville Sound, a smooth, inoffensive wall of music that was put behind every hit artist, had served its purpose well, increasing country music's sales by making it more palatable to urban listeners. Bobby Bare's "Detroit City" and Floyd Cramer's "Last Date" were proof of the Nashville Sound's effectiveness.

One thing that particularly galled Waylon was the way that Nashville session musicians stared down at their music "charts" while they played. The charts were actually a musical shorthand system unique to Nashville studio musicians, who found that the studio shorthand came in handy when they had to do session after session every day.

The number system, which replaced chords with numbers, allowed an entire arrangement to be contained on a single sheet of paper, quickly and concisely.

"The Number System was a survival mechanism at first," said Neal Matthews, Jr., guitarist-arranger-vocalist with the famed Jordonaires quartet, who is credited with creating the numbering system. "We were singing on so many recording sessions in the 1950s that it became a necessity for us" (Nashville *Tennessean*, January 31, 1985). In the early days of Music Row recording, producers frequently expected to tape four to six songs in a three-hour studio session.

The Jordonaires began using the system around 1958, and by 1963, two years before Waylon began recording in Nashville, it was in general use by studio musicians.

The number system was a source of constant irritation to Waylon, who was accustomed to playing with a band who knew his material inside out. He resented the musicians playing with their noses buried in their number charts, seemingly unaware of the singer they were backing.

Waylon won small recognition with his very first RCA releases. The Stockman's Association of the Greater Southwest selected him as "Top New Country and Western Act" of 1965 and gave him their Pioneer Award.

In 1965 Johnny Cash chose Waylon's "A Singing Star's Queen" for his *Everybody Loves a Nut* comedy album. Waylon also had a guest role in the movie *Road to Nashville*, singing "Anita, You're Dreaming" from his second RCA single.

Waylon was delighted to be produced by Chet Atkins, who was already a legendary producer and A&R (Artist and Repertoire) man. Chet became Waylon's friend, and was his most sympathetic producer of the 1965–72 period.

At Waylon's first RCA session, on March 16, 1965, in Nashville, Chet produced Jennings on Harlan Howards' "Another Bridge to Burn," a Jackson King song "Now Everybody Knows," and the King-Bowman tune "I Wonder Just Where I Went Wrong." Most of the Waylors twiddled their thumbs at a nearby motel while Waylon recorded.

Chet let Waylon accompany himself on guitar (as Waylon had been doing for years on stage) on many of his recordings, beginning with Jennings's second session (March 18), which yielded his second RCA single, "Stop the World (And Let Me Off)." Chet let some of the Waylors play on Waylon's early sessions, though it would be ten years before Jennings would be allowed to bring his full stage band into the studio.

"If I had to explain why things were much better with Victor, I guess it was because for one thing I was cutting better records. Plus the label believed in me from the beginning. Like A&M Records—nobody took it seriously as a country label. A&M was just Herb Alpert. I couldn't get the airplay like Victor. Every Country disc jockey will listen to an RCA record, if he's worth his oats. They know the quality is there. Then, too, with Chet's name as producer, they know there's got to be something going for it, at least musically, if not because of the artist" (Grissim).

Chet wasn't crazy about using road musicians in the studio, because that loosened a producer's control over the sound. You knew what you were getting with experienced studio "pickers," as they are called. You could count on cutting X songs in Y number of hours with the pros, and that meant predictable, lean budgets—which labels like. These are the main reasons why even bands such as Alabama still use studio pickers in making Nashville records.

Chet and Waylon had one serious area of disagreement, and that was Waylon's use of uppers, or amphetamines. In several interviews Waylon joked about how Chet "didn't even want to see" an upper. Carl Perkins remarked in an interview that around that time Waylon "would swallow a door knob if you offered him one."

Lucky Moeller, in one of the few sage moves he made regarding Waylon's career, suggested that Waylon wait for a few RCA singles to be released before moving to Nashville. Waylon was still living in Phoenix and playing at J.D.'s when his first RCA single, "That's the Chance I'll Have to Take," hit number forty-nine in mid-1965. His second single, "Stop the World (And Let Me Off)," reached number sixteen that fall, and "Anita, You're Dreaming," which Waylon had written with Don Bowman, rose to number seventeen in early 1966.

In March 1966 RCA released its first Waylon Jennings album, *Folk-Country*. Several writers have alleged that Atkins in his production and choice of an album title was trying to position Waylon for acceptance by a mass audience that reached far beyond country into the folk and pop fields. These writers suggest Atkins tried the same ploy with John Loudermilk, Bobby Bare, and George Hamilton IV. Chet denied having any such plan in mind.

Waylon finally moved to Nashville around April of 1966, about the time of *Folk-Country* and his fourth RCA single, "Time to Bum Again."

Waylon looks different today and sings different songs than he did in 1965, but one thing was obvious on *Folk-Country*, recorded twenty years ago: Jennings had a million-dollar voice. The face that this awesome voice was eclipsed by mundane arrangements and "busy" sound mixes is also apparent, but overall the album is quite good. The album cover shows him as a clean-shaven young man with slicked-back hair, wearing white pants and a nice sports jacket any mother would approve of, and strumming an acoustic guitar.

Folk-Country features one of Waylon's all-time favorite songs, "Look Into My Teardrops," with a heavy bass line, light dobro riffs, and, as with the entire album, a sound that strikes the ear as cluttered. There is a touch of folk in the Jackson King tune "That's the Chance I'll Have to Take," but other than that, the album title has little to do with the Waylon Jennings sound of that time.

After several releases Waylon was ready to move to Nashville. He was also ready to end his marriage to Lynne. By 1966 he was keeping company with Phoenix native Barbara Rood, a pretty blonde from a well-to-do family.

When Jennings finally moved to Nashville, it was Barbara, not Lynne, who moved with him. His brother Tommy, who had come up from Lubbock to join the band as a bass-player in Phoenix, found his own place in Nashville as well.

Shortly after arriving in Nashville, Waylon moved in with Johnny Cash, with whom he would live for approximately the next year and a half.

When Waylon Jennings and Johnny Cash met just over twenty years ago, Jennings was a struggling newcomer to charts and Cash was a superstar, having cut "Ring of Fire," "I Walk the Line," "Folsom Prison Blues," and other hits.

Waylon had met Cash briefly in Phoenix, when Cash was traveling through on a concert tour. He met Johnny again in Nashville in early 1966, when Waylon needed a place to stay and Cash was looking for a roommate. Cash suggested that they stay together.

66

When Waylon moved into the small Fontaine Bleau apartment in the Madison area north of Nashville and split the $150-a-month rent with Johnny, he needed the money he was saving on rent. Cash needed the company, because he had recently divorced and felt miserable over not seeing his daughters. Waylon wasn't great company — more often than not he was hangin' out somewhere in Nashville.

Waylon and Cash had a lot in common. "We were both pretty lost," Waylon said. "We felt pretty sorry for ourselves. Not for each other, for ourselves" (*Door*, December 9–23). Misery loves company.

Barbara Rood rented an apartment below Waylon's, but soon moved back to Phoenix. Waylon and Johnny, constantly pilled out, angry at themselves and often raisin' hell, kept a carpenter busy, kicking down doors and breaking windows and fixtures. Cash did the cooking and Jennings did the tidying up.

Between them, Cash and Jennings were popping a couple of dozen pills a day, though neither ever gave the other a pill or took a pill in front of the other. Cash's addiction to pills had caused his marriage to fall apart. In his misery he turned even more toward pills, uppers and downers.

In his book *Man in Black* (Zondervan, 1975) Cash recalled the time he hid a large supply of Benzedrine (uppers) from Jennings, as well as hundreds of barbiturates (downers). Johnny believed that Waylon didn't know he took pills. As often happened, Cash soon forgot where he had hidden the pills, and got desperate.

"I was frantically looking for the pills one night when Waylon came in. I had the air conditioner out of the window and was taking it apart to look inside when he walked in.

67

" 'What in the world are you doing?' he asked.

" 'I'm trying to fix this air conditioner,' I said.

'See if you can find my pills in there while you're at it,' Waylon grinned."

Jennings still chuckles when he recalls the time he and Cash spent ten hours out in a boat on a lake, supposedly fishing, but in fact never getting so much as a nibble. When it came time to call it a day, Cash couldn't find where he had parked the car! It "must've taken us eight hours to find the damn car," Waylon recalled.

Waylon eventually suggested that Cash find a house of his own, that it might make Cash's ex feel more inclined to let his daughter's visit. Cash took Waylon's advice, and around the spring of 1967 bought the house near a lake in Hendersonville, Tennessee, where he still lives.

Though they were good friends, their difference in musical styles meant Jennings and Cash would not record together for another ten years.

While others were staying safely within country bounds with their choice of song material, Waylon from his earliest RCA recordings was choosing from the Beatles, Rolling Stones, Chuck Berry, Kris Kristofferson, Jimmy Webb, and others, in addition to well-known country writers.

His fourth RCA single, "Time to Bum Again," released in the spring of 1966, had as its flip side "Norwegian Wood," a moody John Lennon-Paul McCartney composition that was avant-garde even for the Beatles, who included it on their *Rubber Soul* album. Chet Atkins, though a proponent of the Nashville Sound, was creative and secure enough to experiment with such tracks — and he let Waylon use a few of the Waylors in the studio.

Waylon's biggest trouble came later, with other producers who were thrown his way.

Nashville in those days was a small community of labels, producers, publishers, studios, booking agents, studio musicians, and songwriters. In some ways the recording artist was low man on the totem pole, expected to play by an intricate set of rules that bound all these entities—and to sing what he was told.

"When I first saw how they were doing it in Nashville, I just couldn't believe it. Rock stars had all kinds of say in their material and production, and here it was in Nashville that country music people were sent into studios to work with musicians they didn't choose, and there were a lot of other people involved who you didn't even know.

"That was lack of respect for country artists. How could you expect somebody's best work on that kind of half-hearted basis?" (*Pittsburgh Press*, February 11, 1982).

Chapter Seven

Fighting the System

In 1966, shortly after moving to Nashville, Waylon landed the lead role in the American International film *Nashville Rebel*, which *Rolling Stone* critic, J. R. Young, described as "one of those raunchy C&W epics seldom seen outside the confederacy or California drive-ins at 4:30 in the morning after 'Hell Bent for Hell on the Hell Machines'." This grade-B dog was produced by Fred Niles Productions "of Hollywood and Chicago."

It is a classic irony in Waylon Jennings's life that his career in Nashville began with a movie role that in many ways foreshadowed the general pattern of disillusionment his life would follow over the next twenty years.

Nashville Rebel, released in February 1967, was billed by its producers as "The story of a young singer's rise to fame, downfall, and climb back up to the top, both in life and in music." A Lucky Moeller PR release at the time said Tex Ritter, playing himself, counsels Jennings in the movie, and that Ritter's character represents "the warmth and heart of the Country Music industry."

Waylon portrayed Arlin Grove, "a young rebel

70

making his way to stardom," according to liner notes written for the soundtrack album by the picture's associate producer. "Success is often followed by the letdown of dark moments, and Arlin, too, experiences this disillusionment and loneliness." Waylon got the role partly through the suggestions of Moeller and Atkins, and worked on it when he was not on the concert trail between April and July 1966. He attended its Nashville premiere in October.

Shot at the Grand Ole Opry and other Nashville locations, with additional scenes shot in Chicago, *Nashville Rebel* also features appearances by Loretta Lynn, Sonny James, the Wilburn Brothers, Porter Wagoner, and others.

A callow Jennings, who had never really worked the road to this point, said in the May 1966 *Music City News*, "I'm really looking forward to working the road. It isn't an easy life, but I don't expect it to be. I'm looking forward to meeting the people. People are really all an entertainer has, and I intend to make time for the folks who have helped me so much.

"I can remember when I was trying to get backstage to see the stars, and I think the biggest thrill of my life was when Billy Walker was real nice to me."

Lucky Moeller got Waylon and his band a total of about $600 a night for bookings in 1966. Waylon's brother Tommy continued to play bass in Waylon's band until 1968, when he left to run Waylon's business and publishing operations.

Waylon's second album, *Leavin' Town,* released in late 1966, built on the success of his first album. *Cash Box* magazine named Waylon the Most Promising Male Vocalist of 1966.

Unfortunately, Waylon's personal life was *not* the most promising. Lynne filed for divorce in early

71

1967, and that October Waylon, thirty, found himself married for the third time. This time he took the vows with Barbara Rood, in a ceremony at the posh home of her millionaire father in Scottsdale, Arizona.

The fact that anyone in his right mind could tell that the Jennings/Rood match wouldn't last didn't phase Waylon. Barbara, an intelligent, pretty blonde from a comfortably wealthy family, was extremely possessive and jealous, and the one way she had of keeping an eye on Waylon—traveling with him on the road—not only bothered him and his band, but also took her away from the comforts of home to which she was accustomed. Barbara was unhappy with and without Waylon.

The Waylors felt that Barbara and her father (who at one point offered to buy out Locky Moeller's contract with Waylon) were trying to "take over," and they resented Barbara's presence. The whole situation became strained. Barbara soon got the message, and though she and Waylon began to relate to each other as friends, their marriage suffered, and it was over in less than two years.

In 1967 Porter Wagoner recorded a Waylon composition "Julie," taking it to the number fifteen spot on *Billboard*'s country singles chart. Jennings released one of his better albums of the period in 1967, *Waylon Sings Ol' Harlan*, in which he sang twelve Harlan Howard songs, including "Heartaches by the Number."

When Waylon appeared on the Grand Ole Opry for the first time in 1967, he came up against yet another crusty Nashville institution. He was informed that his band couldn't include drums, because drum kits simply weren't allowed on the Opry stage. Never mind the fact that they were used on virtually every country record on the charts—Opry tradition was Opry tradition. Waylon was also irked when some full-time Opry artists let it be known that they didn't consider his sound "country" enough.

By late 1968 Waylon's work schedule reportedly kept him on the road twenty-five days a month (three hundred days a year!). He and the Waylors traveled in a bucket-of-nuts-and-bolts bus nicknamed Black Maria. It was utterly and completely black—even its chrome was painted black. His work schedule, combined with his increasing use of pills, took a toll on his songwriting output, a fact that Waylon frankly admitted in more than one interview.

The scores of honky tonks and "skull orchards" that Waylon had to play on the road would test the mettle of any artist. (The worst place, he has said more than once, was a club in Crab Orchard, Kentucky.) Waylon remembered some pretty rough clubs from this time, especially this one in Salisbury, Maryland:

"The first thing that happened when I walked through the door was that somebody shot a cue ball at me. Then on the way to the stage, somebody hit me in the stomach. I was still lookin' around for that guy when another one offered to fight me right on stage.

"I got a little upset and told him to come on up, and Lord, he was a big 'un too. Musta weighed 250 pounds. I was fixin' to wrap that Fender [guitar] right around his head when he climbed on the stage, but they pulled him back before he could get up there" (Roanoke *World-News*, September 25, 1974).

"Then there was a club in Louisville. A guy who usually worked as a bouncer there traded me his girl for my cigarette lighter, and all night long he was tellin' me what a lover she was, puttin' her on my lap.

He was drinkin' and I was humorin' him, y'know, so after it was over, I said, 'Hey, give me my lighter back, you can have your girl back.'

"He handed me my lighter and I said, 'Okay, bye,' and walked about two foot [sic] before I heard some other guy say somethin' about this girl. Her boyfriend hit him, the other guy *shot* him. Didn't shoot him dead, but he got up and walked out drippin' blood" (*Photoplay*, February 1975).

In 1968, Waylon performed on Don Bowman's humorous RCA single, "Ugly Old Gladys Jones," a song he wrote with Bowman back in Phoenix. (Bowman, by then a DJ in California, released a number of comedy and song parody records on RCA.) Waylon also played guitar on albums by Chet Atkins, Harlan Howard, Skeeter Davis, and others in this period.

The early part of that year brought Waylon his first top-five singles, "Only Daddy That'll Walk the Line" (which hit number two) and "Walk on Out of My Mind" (number five).

In 1968 Waylon also started seeing a pretty young singer/songwriter from Mesa, Arizona, named Mirriam Johnson, who was recently divorced from guitar player/early rock instrumentalist Duane Eddy. (Duane, also a Phoenix native, is yet another artist who recommended Waylon to Chet Atkins in 1964.)

Waylon's career gathered momentum slowly, but there was no doubt that he was a special artist. At one point his first four RCA albums were all on the charts.

"Then after a while things started happening fast," Waylon said. "I began spending a lot of time on the road as booking picked up. Like I was on the road three hundred days last year [1968], which meant I had to work just to find time to even record. Right now [1969], I won't be able to record again for another two months at least.

". . . Living that kind of existence can be rough on a person . . . it liked to ruin my mind."

Waylon also complained in print about the pressures he was already feeling as a country performer. He disliked the crowds of fans who beset him after a show, and felt uncomfortable doing all the things country stars were expected to do after the show, such as signing autographs and mingling with the fans.

"It's actually a courtesy thing on the part of the artists, if you want to know the way I feel about it . . . if I don't feel like it, I won't. A lot of people say you owe it to them, but somebody once said, and it's true, that all you owe the people is a good performance, 'cuz that's what they paid to hear. You don't owe them your soul."

In 1968 Waylon's father died of a heart attack . . . his third marriage was falling apart . . . his drug use and an incredibly demanding road schedule were literally wasting him away . . . and he was increasingly unhappy with his treatment by RCA.

Waylon admitted in several interviews around this time that he took pills, saying they gave him the energy he needed for concerts and offset the boredom of the road. "I really don't think I've improved over the last two years. I've rushed sessions and had so many things to do" he said in 1969 (Grissim).

Waylon also admitted it was a great strain on him to fight the system in Nashville; "It takes a lot of strain and guts to fight the system. . . . You see, I'm considered outside the system. If I win, they feel like they've lost. . . . I don't want to fight with them. I don't want to argue with them. It's just that I'm very vulnerable in this position. But you also find that vulnerability gives you a lot of strength.

"It's always hard, going up against tradition or whatever. But to me, it's worth it. For the bottom line on everything is that the artistic urge has to be handled as carefully as sex" (*Miami News,* October 24, 1975).

Waylon's taping on March 5, 1969, of the "Joey Bishop Show" was his first appearance on a national talk show—and his first experience with what he felt was TV's stupid portrayal and treatment of country artists. On the "Joey Bishop Show," Waylon was brought on stage during the last five minutes of the show and told where to stand, what to sing, and then to get off the stage.

"Joey Bishop and his big baloney about how he loved country music . . . that's the biggest joke in the world. I played his show and I tried to get him to take my part off 'cause I stood there singing madder than a son of a bitch. I told him what I thought about him and the whole bunch of them. I told him, . . . 'If you're going to present country music, present it right. Don't come on like a big bullshitter' " (*Door,* December 9–23, 1971).

By late 1969 Jennings had appeared on these TV shows as well: "Hee Haw," the "Glen Campbell Show," ABC-TV's "Anatomy of Pop," the "Bobby Lord Show," and "American Swingaround" (Chicago), as well as guesting on the Grand Ole Opry.

Waylon's show in those days ran about as long as it does today, fifty minutes. He allowed himself little time between numbers to talk with his audience. Critics noted that he came across on stage more forcefully than other artists in his category, and that his voice colored his music with a sense of purpose and depth that it otherwise lacked.

In April 1969, writing in BMI's *Many Worlds of*

Music magazine, *Los Angeles Times* music critic Robert Hilburn wrote: "In recent months, Jennings has established himself as the most exciting new country singer in years. He features a hard, driving sound that has much of the same earthy appeal as the early country-rock numbers." Jennings told Hilburn, "There has been a big change in country music. At one time, it was considered too far out if you had a minor chord in a song. We have moved a long way since then."

In early 1969 Waylon met with Johnna Yurcic, a man who would go to work full-time with Waylon a few years later. In Gallup, New Mexico, that year Catholic priest Father Dunstan Schmidlin held many dances for native American Indians on reservations in the area. He hired an assistant, Yurcic, to help book talent for the dances in Gallup, and at other reservations in New Mexico and Arizona.

Over the next two and half years Yurcic booked Waylon for many concerts for Indians and the underprivileged. Johnna says Waylon was getting from $1,700 to $2,500 a show then, depending on the day of the week and the time of the year. Waylon and Johnna got on well, and Yurcic eventually joined Waylon's road crew in 1972.

Also in early 1969, shortly after playing a reservation concert, Waylon returned to Nashville and recorded a song with The Kimberleys, a vocal group whose show he had seen in Las Vegas. It was an unusual move for a Nashville act to use a folk-oriented vocal backup, and even more unusual to pick a pop song such as "MacArthur Park" to record, but Waylon made both unusual moves. "A country person, no matter where you're at, can relate to 'MacArthur Park,' because there ain't nothin' more country than a yellow cotton dress or old men in the park playin' dominoes or checkers," he said (*Popular Music & Society*, No. 3, 1974).

In July of 1969 Waylon stunned the country music industry—and probably himself—by winning a Grammy for Best Vocal Group Performance for "MacArthur Park." Waylon's version of the song only reached number twenty-three on the country charts and ninety-three on the pop charts, and many thought it was not really suited to Waylon's style—but it won a Grammy all the same. "We got a Grammy for the song," Waylon told *Country Side*, but . . . neither field accepted it. No field really accepted it as one of their songs." (True to form, in a 1969 concert Waylon forgot the words to the song that won him a Grammy.)

Waylon was featured on his own Metromedia TV special, 1969's "Love of the Common People," named for a moderately successful Jennings album and single released in 1967. In 1969 he also sang six Shel Silverstein songs on the United Artists soundtrack to the mediocre movie *Ned Kelly*, in which Mick Jagger played a famous Australian outlaw. Jagger and Kris Kristofferson also sang on the soundtrack.

In 1969, Richie Albright, who had been Waylon's drummer since 1964 in Phoenix, left the Waylors. He had been dissatisfied ever since leaving Phoenix—he felt they should have stayed there and taken another year or two to polish and tighten their sound. But he kept in touch with Waylon and rejoined the group in 1972.

Once Waylon had become an established RCA artist, inferior product began to slip out from his past. There was the Bat bootleg single, the J.D.'s LP, and then Decca's release of ten of the J.D.'s tracks on a Vocalion album. A&M jumped on the bandwagon by releasing its *Don't Think Twice* album in 1970. Waylon liked the music on the A&M album and cooperated with the project by posing for a cover photo.

Waylon's brooding but sensitive sound was attracting national attention, both in general interest publications and in the pop press. *Seventeen* magazine soon came to call him the "Humphrey Bogart of country music," whatever that means. Waylon sang in the contemporary country vein, but RCA didn't know what it had on its hands, or how to label him. Waylon's music avoided the uptight, self-pitying, morality-preaching songs that so many other artists used as standard fare.

On October 26, 1969, Waylon took one of the most important steps of his life—he married his fourth and present wife, Jessi Colter. Shortly before Waylon married Jessi, Chet Atkins signed her to RCA, and Waylon and Chet produced her first album, *A Country Star Is Born*. Neither the album nor the singles pulled from it made a dent on the charts.

Jessi did record two successful duets with Waylon, though—1970's "Suspicious Minds" and 1971's "Under Your Spell Again." (She would make her own mark on music history with her Capitol releases a few years later.) Jessi appeared on the covers of Waylon's albums *Singer of Sad Songs* (1970) and *Cedartown, Georgia* (1971).

Waylon was generally happy with Chet, though Chet didn't latch on to Waylon's unique sound. ". . . He encouraged me to play guitar on my own records and what have you. As far as Chet Atkins, I have nothing but respect for him. [E]specially when I changed A&R men, a lot of times I'd cut records and I'd come back in and they had a little bitty horn here and a little bitty guitar there that I didn't hardly recognize . . ." (*Popular Music & Society*, No. 3, 1974).

Waylon became quite unhappy around 1970 when Chet's administrative duties with RCA increased, and he was forced to reduce his incredibly heavy production schedule. Waylon, like other RCA artists, was from then on handled by various assistant producers, such as Danny Davis, Ronnie Light, Felton Jarvis, Jack Clement, Bob Ferguson, and others.

Back then (as still happens to many artists today), the producer picked the songs, hired bored but competent studio pickers to cut three or four of those songs in a three-hour studio session, had the artist sing a hasty vocal track, and then sent the singer away so the track could be "sweetened" with additional accompaniment.

The boundary between pop and country was becoming more vague, due in large part to the new breed of songwriters who were filtering into Music City. These writers weren't all farm boys. They were Army brats, Rhodes scholars, former journalists, ex-pop band members — writers who didn't feel obliged to stay within the strict guidelines of the Nashville Sound of the day.

Nashville was even airlifting in pop singers with no country leanings, such as Perry Como and Rosemary Clooney, to get the Nashville Sound assembly-line treatment, a neat, cost-efficient kit complete with number charts, country lyrics, country sidemen, and a country producer.

Willie Nelson later recalled being put off by the Nashville way of making records. "I'd get nervous. I just didn't feel comfortable in that kinda situation. You'd walk into the studio and they'd put six guys behind you who'd never seen your music before, and it's impossible to get the feel of it in a three-hour session. That was true for me, at least" (*New York Times Magazine*, March 26, 1978).

Waylon's long-running feud with the Nashville establishment was really over style, accompaniment, and presentation. The question Waylon asked was, "Whose music is this, mine or yours?" Waylon was well aware this his music, which had seemed so vital on stage in Phoenix, was now getting the same whining steel and familiar guitar licks that all the other mass-produced sessions generated in Nashville. Waylon's sound was country with a mean rockabilly bite, a pounding bass line topped with Waylon's chicken-pickin', stutterin' style of lead guitar play.

"They wouldn't let me pick my own songs. They wouldn't let me use my own band in the studio. They would bring all their buddy musicians in and listen to their advice on how to make a record, but not mine.

"I'd cut a basic track, and by the time they were through adding stuff, I didn't even recognize it any more. They also complained about the way I dressed, and that my hair was too long, though it was really pretty short in those days.

"A lot of it, though, was my own fault," Waylon admits. "I wasn't *ready* for success back then. When I was on drugs, my attention span was pretty short. Sometimes it was hard to even talk to me" (*Genesis*, December 1984).

In these early years RCA had Waylon popping out albums as fast as most performers put out singles. The early Waylon Jennings albums produced by Chct Atkins were well received by buyers and critics, and they charted respectably. But between 1966 and 1970 Waylon churned out a dozen albums, and he knew that the quality of his music was suffering.

For Waylon these years were marked by frustration

and despair. He had left A&M in 1965 to work with Chet Atkins at RCA, but by 1970 he was being shuffled off on less capable producers. He felt that he was misunderstood by RCA, and the road was sapping him of his fighting strength. His self-destructive drug habit wasn't helping, either.

Waylon was attracting attention, but none of his first nine RCA albums made it into the top ten on sales charts. One reason he wasn't making the leap into the rank of superstar may have been his personal appearances. Waylon did not have what most country fans thought a "star's" stage show and personality ought to be.

Some thought Waylon's shows were too loud, too close to rock 'n roll. Whatever one thought of Waylon's musical style, there was no denying that Waylon was inconsistent in concert, brilliant one night and seemingly disinterested the next (drugs may have been a big factor in this). Many disliked the fact that Waylon didn't stick around after his concerts to chat and sign autographs. Waylon often forgot lyrics and ad-libbed verses on stage, a byproduct of his refusal to go with a formula song lineup, and probably of his pill habit as well.

As the 1960s drew to a close, Waylon sensed that his career had reached a plateau. His albums began to lack excitement, power, and originality. There was an occasional gem, but for the most part his albums belonged where they wound up—in the cutout bins.

Most of all, Waylon was acutely aware that he didn't fit into the Nashville "mold."

At A&M Waylon had been too country for the label to market. Ironically, he puzzled RCA because the label felt he wasn't country enough. "There used to be a guy with RCA that would come in and say, 'You just be quiet, and we will take care of this. We know what we are doing about these records.' Now where is that coming from—he knows what he is doing about MY music? Telling me what to release, and then he sits there and pats his foot to the wrong beat. . . .And he whistled with a Yankee accent.

"Nobody is going to make me change anything about my music. I ain't saying that is the easiest way to go. But I had to do it that way. And I'm glad I did" (*Country Music*, January/February 1979).

Chapter Eight

"All I Wanted to Do Was Survive"

Early 1972 found Waylon Jennings laying in a hospital, sick with hepatitis and near bankruptcy. The thirty-four-year-old singer looked at his life and music career and wondered what the hell had gone wrong. He was spending almost three hundred days a year on the road and he felt like it was about to kill him — that and the pills and cocaine.

Ironically, he was near breaking through to superstardom. He'd had more than half a dozen top-five hits, and would soon unleash a string of number ones — but he was half a million dollars in debt, and at a physical and emotional lowpoint.

Waylon's drummer and close friend since the Phoenix days, Richie Albright, was still gone, and Waylon felt like he was battling The System alone. He especially resented the "Dear Artist" form letters that he got from RCA. It was just one more way they had of making him feel like a number in a computer.

Waylon spent a lot of time thinking about his situation: "I spent a lot of years, scattered," Waylon said, "going through a lot of changes, going through a lot of things that it took me a long time to learn weren't what I wanted or needed. I think the thing that was a blessing in disguise, was that I got sick . . . , and it gave me a chance to kinda look back and see where I had been, and wonder where I was headed" (*Country Song Roundup*, March 1975).

RCA released a dozen Waylon Jennings albums between 1966 and the close of 1969. Waylon scored hit singles, a Grammy award, and consistent (though not blockbuster) album sales. But he knew that his *real* sound, his vital, raw stage sound, was hopelessly buried in the bland, over-produced Nashville Sound style favored by the various staff producers assigned to Waylon.

Speaking of producers, Waylon got dizzy watching them come and go. After Chet reduced his production load around 1970, Waylon encountered a new face behind the control board almost every time he went into the studio. His albums released between 1970 and 1972 credit six different producers.

Waylon was ready to quit the business. He couldn't do it *their* way any longer, and was about to pack it up. He wanted off the merry-go-round. He thought about going back to being a disc jockey, and about learning to play guitar better so he could make a living doing session work. "I didn't really know what to do," he said. "I just felt all burned out inside. I was really down and it felt like people were still trying to kick me."

Waylon knew that his attitude toward the Nashville system made him look like a rebel, but he didn't see himself that way. All he wanted was the control that any artist would expect over his creation. "I couldn't conform to the way they did things. I never said they were wrong. I just said it was wrong for me. The thing is, they always told me they knew better. I believed them for a while, but then I could see they didn't know better" (*Los Angeles Times*, November

19, 1978).

Waylon got so fed up watching the musicians play with their heads buried in their chord charts that one time he brought a gun — it wasn't loaded — with him to the studio, and after several run-throughs of a song he took it out and said, "The first guy I see looking at that chart . . . I'm going to shoot his fingers off." They listened to the music.

Waylon was unhappy with his treatment by RCA and the Nashville music establishment, with his own records, and with his finances. The money he made on the road wasn't great, and much of it went to pay the costs of being on the road. But the fans and press were beginning to discover his music, and they liked it.

Waylon's records were well received, but he knew he could do better, and he grew more despondent. His singles had flirted with the top ten on country charts every since 1966, and now he was picking up the tempo. "Good Hearted Woman," which he wrote with Willie Nelson, went to number three in 1972, and four of his next five singles would go top ten.

The country music scene was changing. John Hartford's "Gentle on My Mind" smash for Glen Campbell turned the nation's attention to Nashville as a music source again. Kris Kristofferson's songwriting success with "Me and Bobby McGee," "For the Good Times," "Help Me Make It Through the Night," and other songs pointed out that country music was capable of changing and maturing with the times.

Waylon had never been allowed to produce one of his own albums at RCA, though he had recorded more than twenty for the label, and was by now quite capable of offering creative input.

Around November 1970, legendary steel guitar player Ralph Mooney joined the Waylors, after meeting Waylon at a party while Jennings was on a tour of Texas. Waylon admitted that he had never been a fan of the steel guitar, but was in awe of Mooney, having loved Ralph's previous work with country artist Buck Owens and others. Waylon was so nervous about asking Mooney to work for him that at the party it took him several hours to work up the courage to ask him to join the Waylors!

Mooney thinks quite a lot of Waylon, too: "One of my best souvenirs is a note which Waylon shoved under my motel room door after we'd had a really good soundin' night down in Odessa, Texas. The note says, 'Moon, you're the greatest there ever was' " (Louisville, Kentucky *Courier-Journal,* November 15, 1975).

Waylon visited the U.K. and countries in northern Europe for the first time in 1971-72. His first appearance at the International Festival of Country Music in Wembley, England, in 1972 was marred by a faulty sound system, but British fans were nonetheless delighted to get their first sight of Waylon "live."

That same year Waylon again admitted in print that he was weary of the road: "It's hard to keep your head up all the time when you're traveling and all you see is the roof of some motel room and an audience full of strange faces. I guess the impersonal part gets to me" (*Door,* December 9–23). He admitted that he continued to take pills, too.

Around this time he was doing about two hundred shows a year, usually making about $1,750 a night. His more successful records sold 100,000 to 200,000 copies, even today an impressive number for an up-and-coming country artist.

In late 1969 and early 1970 he recorded *Singer of Sad Songs* at the RCA studios in Los Angeles. Despite the fact that he had throat trouble, Waylon was pushed through marathon recording sessions, recording eighteen hours straight at one point. For Waylon it was just one more example of how the artist was regarded as a pawn by the game players, the producers and label executives. Rushing sessions to meet deadlines was not unusual for producers who work with Waylon. "It was mass production, like an assembly line—four songs in three hours. I did eight damn songs one night in three hours." Lee Hazelwood's production added an almost bizarre edge to Waylon's music.

An important media milestone in Waylon's career came on December 9, 1971, when *Rolling Stone* magazine printed an article by J. R. Young titled "The Monster Voice of Waylon Jennings." Young told of a dull winter day when he happened across a Jennings album in his collection. It was 1970's *Singer of Sad Songs,* and it knocked Young out:

"The first thing you hear is this man singing, a *man* man the likes of which rock hasn't heard in a long time. What pipes. No kid's stuff here, boy. Just the real thing. Two weeks later I had the first fourteen albums."

Young went on to describe Waylon's sound: "RCA labeled it 'Country-Folk' at first, and then finally let it ride as straight country. It was a soft country sound, melodic and reminiscent of early Marty Robbins. Very tasty stuff. . . . Word is that if Waylon Jennings isn't already a country superstar, he soon well be."

It seems like the closer Waylon got to stardom, the worse he felt. The past few years on the road and his fight with the system had taken a lot out of him. He saw his money draining away—in fact, he lost money playing some dates. Waylon was going broke, to the tune of almost half a million dollars.

Waylon was suddenly struck down by infectious hepatitis, which he believes he contracted from the drinking water on one of the Navajo reservations he had played in New Mexico. His illness was made worse by his drug abuse.

For 1972's *Ladies Love Outlaws,* Waylon finally succeeded in blending his Waylors with the Nashville session men on his tracks, and in picking some more custom-fitting song material, such as Hoyt Axton's "Never Been to Spain," Alex Harvey's "Delta Dawn," and the Lee Clayton title cut.

Waylon has never been entirely happy with the album, because his hospitalization prevented him from putting the finishing touches he had on mind on the tracks. He thought "Never Been to Spain" was "a really bad cut. . . . I didn't get to put the harmony on it like I wanted."

On this album even Waylon's appearance changed, signaling some deeper changes to come. Where Waylon's photos formerly showed a man with greased-back hair, clean-shaven and well groomed, they now showed a man with longer, unkempt hair falling forward on his face, a beard, faded jeans, boots, and turquoise chains around his neck.

Richie Albright returned to the band in April of 1972 after an absence of more than two years and introduced Waylon to artist manager Neil Reshen. Getting away from Nashville had given Richie the chance to see how the folks in L. A. and New York did things in the rock music business, how well they treated artists (compared to the country music scene), and how efficiently tours were handled. Richie and Neil thought some of the same measures could be put into practice in country.

"Richie told me, 'Let's give it one more run.' He told me he'd come back with me and if it didn't work this time, we'd both go back to Phoenix or some-where and get a sit-down job and take it easy."

Waylon spoke with Reshen and found him to be a street-wise, fast-talking man who reminded him of "a short Abraham Lincoln with a dishonest face." Neil was Waylon's bulldog on a chain, just what he needed to deal with RCA and Nashville at that point in his career. "He fought those record companies like a mad dog," Waylon said in amazement.

Waylon agreed that very day to let Neil be his manager. Later that day Neil and Waylon bumped into Willie Nelson, who also decided to give Neil a try with his career. "He had nothing to lose — what did he have to start with anyway?" Reshen said. Neil told Waylon that "if I can do five percent of what I think I can do, it'll be one hundred percent more than anyone else ever did for you."

Waylon was about thirty-five and at the end of his rope when he signed on with Reshen. After about twenty years connected with the music business he was sick, broke, and under the control of people who didn't understand his music. Almost immediately Reshen helped Waylon get better advances from RCA, a higher royalty rate, and control over his production and other facets of his work.

Reshen lost no time in raising Waylon's profile with the urban audience, and in reorganizing Waylon's business and record label affairs. "Everybody had a piece of him, eighteen different ways," Neil said. There were states Waylon couldn't visit because of alimony suits filed by his three ex-wives. He owed Lucky and RCA money that they had advanced him.

Neil settled Waylon's alimony suits, renegotiated his RCA contract, and eventually succeeded in prying Waylon loose from Lucky Moeller, whose book-ing agency was slowly going down the drain from mismanagement anyway. For the time being Reshen got an immediate increase in Waylon's concert fee, from $1,750 to $2,500.

Early in 1973 Reshen had Waylon play Max's Kansas City, a New York pop club. Standing on stage, still weak from his bout with hepatitis and looking tired and raunchy in the harsh lights, Waylon growled into the microphone on opening night: "I hope you all like what we do. If you don't, don't ever come to Nashville. We'll kick the hell out of you!"

Reshen also had Waylon tape a "Midnight Special" TV segment and perform at the Palomino and Troubadour clubs in Los Angeles. In the audience at his Troubadour show were such stars as Neil Diamond (who would write the liner notes for a Waylon LP in 1975), Bob Dylan, and Cher. The 1973-74 period was a great one for Jennings with regard to exposure in the popular press — *Penthouse, Playboy,* the *Los Angeles Times, Rolling Stone, Newsweek,* and other major publications were singing praises of Waylon and his music.

Waylon was bothered by people who turned their nose up at his effort to appeal to a market that was larger than the traditional country market. "What you might call cross over, I call expanding the audience," he retorted. Country music's audience was expanding too. Radio WHN-New York converted to a country format in 1973, as KLAC-Los Angeles had done the previous year.

Reshen's promotional tactics were working. On February 10, 1973, the *Los Angeles Time*'s Robert Hilburn, long a fan of Waylon's, wrote in an article titled "Time for a Jennings Breakthrough?": "It may finally be time for Jennings, one of the most exciting country-based singers in years, to break through to the wider popularity that has so long been predicted for him."

Reshen, who was only about thirty-three when he took charge of Waylon, started in the early 1960s with a management company that handled the business affairs of such pop acts as Sam the Sham and the Pharaohs, Tommy James and the Shondells, Mary Wells, and others. He sold that business and became a VP with Paramount Records, but eventually went back into the management business for himself.

Skilled in accounting and artist management, Neil was familiar with the confusing language of music contracts. He relished his role as Waylon's bulldog, and he was only too willing to dig his teeth into anyone who bothered his artist. Waylon wasn't yet cutting gold or platinum records, but he had enough potential for Reshen to use it as leverage for getting an advance and other concessions to re-sign with RCA.

Reshen's negotiating strategy with RCA was simple—he threatened to take Waylon off the record label if RCA didn't give him what he wanted. Reshen had RCA over a barrel, because he had discovered that the label had not picked up its option to keep Waylon on the roster in 1972.

During one of his talks with an RCA executive, Waylon pointing to Willie Nelson's picture on the executive's wall and said 'You blew it with him, hoss, don't blow it with me.' Willie had already left RCA after several years of frustrations that were similar to Waylon's.

The threat to defect won Waylon and Neil RCA's assurance of better promotion of Waylon's releases, and opened the door for the gradual turnover of artistic control to Jennings. These concessions came only after several rounds of tense negotiations, one of which Waylon describes: ". . . [R]ight in the middle of one of the things where we were negotiating in Chet Atkins's office, [Reshen] stopped [talking], and they stopped, and nobody would say anything 'cause the first one to say anything was going to lose. And I sat there for about as long as I could stand it and then I reached over to this little bowl of peanuts, and I said, 'Chet, what kinds of peanuts are these?' Neil looked at me like he could kill me" (Bane).

In the end, RCA gave Waylon a substantial bonus for re-signing. Waylon said it was more money than he'd ever seen. Jennings recalled that when one of the RCA executives in the room asked if there were anything special he'd like to do with the money, he replied that he'd like to start his own record label. Somebody in the back of the room yelled, "Told you he was crazy!"

Reshen also helped Waylon establish an independent production company, WGJ (for Waylon Goddamn Jennings) Productions, which contracted to provide RCA with a stated number of sides per year. The lines of responsibility were clearly drawn: Waylon created, RCA promoted and sold. Waylon also had control over advertising and promotion budgets. After the contract was signed Chet Atkins walked up to Waylon and said, "You've got a better contract than me, and I've been with the company for twenty-five years!"

The new arrangement delighted Waylon. Things were finally the way he wanted them with RCA. He was responsible for his own product. "When you're an entertainer, if you have no control over what's happening to you it can drive you crazy," he told *Popular Music & Society* (No. 3, 1974).

At the time Waylon thought the world of Reshen. "Neil is a genius. Me and Willie were through. We were up against a brick wall. Neil took us and fed us and loaned us money and didn't know if he was ever gonna get it back. He had faith in us when it was hard to find anyplace to put faith" (*Country Music People*, May 1979).

Neil welcomed the challenge of working with a nonconformist artist such as Waylon. Referring to what the industry considered "difficult" artists, Reshen said, "I only want to handle those. I only want those who have been around and the type who, if they could find direction, would be great. If you can get the confidence of these people, you'll never lose them."

Neil had his wish — he worked with such "difficult" artists as jazz great Miles Davis, and country music's Johnny Paycheck, David Allan Coe, and others, in addition to Nelson and Jennings.

Reshen worked his Media Consulting Corp. out of Danbury, Connecticut. An outspoken man, he gladly took credit for all that he accomplished — and more. He told his local newspaper (*New Times*, September 14, 1975) that, "The fact that a Jewish city slicker is deeply involved with the mechanics of country music is no mean feat. We've expanded the whole area of country music. They were traditionally treated like black artists. But there are more artists like Waylon Jennings who are rebels."

After gaining control, Waylon lost little time in bringing the Waylors into the studio with him, and in doing more of the guitar playing and vocal harmony himself.

The 1973 albums *Lonesome, On'ry and Mean* and *Honky Tonk Heroes* were largely produced by Waylon, and proved that new creative juices were flowing.

Lonesome began to fashion the trademark lean, muscular Jennings sound that shows respect for country tradition while setting new parameters, exploring new topics and shades of feeling. Waylon's sound became leaner, cleaner, with more up-front vocals, less reverb and clutter. His vocals had more snarl and bite, and the sound was more focused, with new texture added to guitar sounds. The sound was raw and crude — but more exciting, as on the ballad "Pretend I Never Happened." "Good Time Charle's Got the Blues" is done with heavier beat and quicker tempo than the original pop hit, with dobro, acoustic guitar, and vocal harmony by Waylon. This album features music more on the edge, more reflective of the stage experimentation that Waylon had always had with his live show.

Waylon's music was showing what he calls his "footprints," or personal style. The *Lonesome* album cover displayed Waylon wearing a goatee, with long, disheveled hair and a menacing look.

The first album over which Waylon had complete artistic control was 1973's *Honky Tonk Heroes*, which drew almost entirely from the song repertoire of Billy Joe Shaver. Co-produced by Tompall Glaser, Ken Mansfield, and Ronnie Light, the collection of modern-day cowboy songs also included Waylon's own composition "Willie the Wandering Gypsy and Me."

The album cover represented a departure from Waylon's past RCA product. The sepia photograph showed Waylon and his band drinking beer on stage. The musicians shown here would form the nucleus of the Waylors for the next few years: Richie Albright, drums; Ralph Mooney, steel guitar; Bee Spears, bass; Don Brooks, harmonica; and Jerry Gropp and Larry Whitmore, rhythm guitars.

"To look back on it now, that album was really ragged," Waylon said. "But it was sensational. A song like 'Ain't No God in Mexico' is just me and Randy Scruggs and a drummer and bass. That's all. That's a lot of real simple stuff. But at the time it was very loose, a real honky tonk hero sound. It sounded like a bunch of cowboys playin'. And it was supposed to sound like that" (*Houston Chronicle*, September 7, 1975).

The album drew praise from critics, though some were disconcerted by the album cover and the different direction the album took. It only reached number 14 on *Billboard*'s country album chart, but today *Honky Tonk Heroes* is recognized as one of the landmark albums in Waylon's career—and in country music's modern history.

Waylon's music had always avoided traditional country themes of drinkin', slipping around back alleys with someone else's wife, or catching your wife slipping around back alleys with someone else. Instead Waylon's music dealt with self-doubt, coming from the soul of an uneasy wanderer alienated by today's fast times. Now his music had more emotional impact, showing a definite influence of early rock music's beat and energy.

The rock influence in Waylon's sound drew flak from country purists and stodgy traditionalists. But Waylon has always stayed within the bounds of country music—it's just that he does it his way. "I couldn't go pop with a mouthful of firecrackers. Merle Haggard's drummer told me that once, and it's true.

". . . Instruments don't make country. We're entitled to a heavy rock beat if it complements our songs. Or if we want to use a kazoo played through a sewer pipe, all right too. Why should we lock ourselves in?" (*Country Music*, April 1973).

"Everybody has ideas of how I *should* sound

instead of how I *did* sound. Now I'm just going to go ahead and do my thing. It's not the instrument or the arrangement that makes country music, it's the soul and the performance. Otherwise, Dean Martin could be the biggest country singer in the world" (*Playboy*, October 1973).

In May 1973, Waylon performed in concert with the Grateful Dead and the Allman Brothers at Kezar Stadium in San Francisco. The show was a success, and Waylon was amazed to experience first-hand how they handled stars and backstage arrangements in the rock world. Flowers were sent to his trailer, and there were huge buffets with steaks, appetizers, drinks, and other refreshments for all the musicians.

Waylon developed a deep mistrust of TV executives in the early 1970s, after a series of fiascos that accompanied his appearances on major talk and variety shows.

In 1973 he left the set of the Dean Martin summer replacement show when "They wanted me to sit on a horse and sing 'We Had It All' — a love ballad — and leave off the first two lines. It just didn't make sense. I don't think they [TV producers and directors] understand our music or respect us as artists."

Waylon taped a segment for "Midnight Special," but then was surprised to learn he would not be allowed to re-do any of his songs or to see the finished product. With the help of a lawyer he finally gained some artistic control, and was able to correct some of the audio problems (including feedback) that had plagued the taping.

While he was making all the other career changes, Waylon also tried to switch from Lucky Moeller's booking agency to the more cosmopolitan William Morris Agency, which had recently opened an office in Nashville. In fact, on July 24, 1973, the Nashville

Tennessean reported that Waylon had made the switch. But Moeller, whose agency was in a severe decline at the time (it would soon be out of business), maintained his grasp on Waylon and two days later the same paper let it be known that Lucky still had Jennings under contract.

It took another two years for Neil to finally get Waylon away from Lucky. Jennings then signed on with the Glasers' Nova agency for a while, and later began to handle his own concert bookings through an in-house operation called Utopia Productions.

In a mid-1973 Associated Press interview Waylon spoke his mind on several topics:

On crossing over: "If our audience has broadened, it's not because I've changed, but because people are listening and finding they don't have a hayseed hanging out of their mouths. Also people want truth, and country music is that if it's nothing else."

On the music business: "It's a frustrating business. There's excitement when you cut a record and two days later you look around and there's nothing going. It's continual uppers and downers.

Waylon enjoyed telling of the time an RCA executive asked him when he was going to start recording some *country* music. Waylon's reply was, "You're one of the problems we got, because you don't know what it is."

After nearly twenty years of singing and playing for a living, Waylon Jennings was being discovered by a nation of country music fans. Reshen's business savvy, Jessi's stabilizing force, and his growing success as an artist should have meant a completely happy life for him, but his drug habit still prevented that. More on that later.

In an interview printed in August 19, 1974, Atlanta *Constitution*, Waylon said: "Hey hoss, it's ten times better than it used to be. We've doubled our income in the last year, and with this band, I'm more into playin' than I've ever been. This is a hell of a group."

Media coverage again picked up, as Waylon was featured in the *New York Times*, *Newsweek*, the *New Yorker*, and other major publications, which began to refer to him as a "country maverick."

After sixteen years of recording Waylon logged his first number-one song in *Billboard* magazine with mid-1974's "This Time." The album of the same title featured friend Willie Nelson, who co-produced the LP and could be heard harmonizing and playing guitar, and included four Willie Nelson songs, "Pick Up the Tempo," "Heaven or Hell," "It's Not Supposed to Be That Way," and "Walkin'." Waylon didn't know that Willie had already recorded those songs for his *Phases and Stages* album on Atlantic. Waylon said Willie's "Pick Up the Tempo" was "more or less about me and him and our struggles along the way with our music."

Some critics feel that 1974's *This Time* is one of Waylon's best albums. *Stereo Review* (Oct. 1976) said it is "essentially about feelings . . . and it eloquently asserts that it's all right for cowboys to have them. Also, it catches Waylon at his sharpest musically. . . ." The sound is low-key and unassuming, but there are flashes of genius throughout. It's an early version of the low-key, late-night music that Willie cashed in on later in the '70's.

Waylon was listed as sole producer for the first time on his second album of 1974, *Waylon, the Ramblin' Man*. The Waylors joined top Nashville pickers on this album to record such songs as Don Williams's "Amanda," Greg Allman's rock hit "Midnight Rider," and Waylon's own "Rainy Day Woman," in addition to the title cut.

Waylon's next single, "I'm a Ramblin' Man," was another number one country song, and it also reached the seventies on the pop charts. The number-one singles "This Time" and "I'm a Ramblin' Man" started a hot streak on the charts that would lay the base for the "superstardom" Waylon would achieve by the late 1970s. From mid-1974 through the present he would become a fixture in the country top ten, with almost a dozen number-one singles, pop cross-over hits, and hit albums along the way.

Reshen made a big difference in Waylon's life when he helped Jennings get rid of Black Maria, the rolling slum of a bus with more than a million miles on its odometer, and get a new $120,000 Silver Eagle bus that set the pace for the industry, complete with Spanish leather seats, gold water faucets, refrigerators, rust-colored corduroy chairs, Waylon's own room with a king-sized bed, televisions, state-of-the-art sound equipment, and other comforts of a fine home. It even had a star with the name "Hank" on the restroom door.

In 1975 RCA released Waylon's *Dreaming My Dreams*, an album that Jennings co-produced with Jack Clement. It includes Waylon's own ruggedly individualistic "Are You Sure Hank Done It This Way?" which reached number one as a single. It is an evocative tune that lay the business on the line as no other Waylon Jennings song had before. Clement, one of the most inventive producers Waylon has worked with, couched the singer's unusual vocals in striking instrumentation, including cellos on "Let's All Help the Cowboys (Sing the Blues)."

The title song, though a love ballad, can also easily be interpreted in light of Waylon's striving for artistic career goals. Clement, a brilliant producer, introduced subtlety and understatement to Waylon's music, and the effect was splendid.

Waylon sported a beard and an "alternative" dress style, as did Willie, and the elements were shifting into place for the explosion of the "outlaw" phase of Waylon's career. The music and image were there — all it needed was a bit of marketing, which is something RCA has always done well.

For Waylon, along with the career control and musical freedom came new pressure — the pressure of knowing everyone is watching, and of taking the entire responsibility for booking, publishing, recording, and career direction. "I'd renegotiated my contract and I was the first one to come up with that artistic freedom and control thing. I know they wanted me to succeed and yet, I know they wanted me to blow it in another way, too" (*Houston Chronicle*, September 7, 1975).

"They say that I beat the system. I didn't do that. The system was after my ass. You know, it's like they were afraid of me, and the whole thing is, the system — it don't know when to quit. There's nothing human about it. It runs itself" (*Gallery*, January 1984).

"I couldn't conform. I wasn't understood and some of it was maybe my fault — drugs, that stuff. They thought I was out to destroy, when all I wanted to do was survive."

Chapter Nine

Meet the Outlaws

A trend was underway in Nashville in the early 1970s, a movement toward presenting real-life, unpolished emotions in country music. Like Waylon, a number of other writers and artists were defying the Nashville System with their music and personal styles, though none (except for Willie) to Waylon's degree.

Country music's "outlaw" movement began in the early 1970s when Waylon, Willie, and a few other country artists simply decided to jump off the Nashville Sound assembly line. These musicians were convinced that there was *another* way to do things, a way outside of the existing Nashville power structure.

The outlaws were country artists who looked and sounded different from other artists. They had long hair and wore jeans all the time. They played Fender Telecaster guitars that they strapped on rock-style, and plugged their guitars into high-voltage amps. They told their drummers to play with a heavy beat, and they stood there under those bright blue stage lights singing straight-from-the-heart lyrics, not giving a damn about tradition or the Grand Ole Opry.

What these artists wanted was what rock artists

had, and what record buyers probably assume all recording artists have anyway: the right to pick their own songs, choose their own studio musicians, and control other creative areas that artists *ought* to control.

Waylon was feeling more confident by the mid-1970s with Neil Reshen as his manager, getting better bookings through his own Utopia (and the Glasers' Nova Agency), his new bus, better advance money and other concessions from RCA—simply more control over his music, his business and his career.

Waylon had long since let his pompadour grow long and shaggy and had grown a beard. He, Willie, and a number of other artists were finding a loyal following in the record-buying public and the press.

In 1972 Waylon recorded a Lee Clayton song called "Ladies Love Outlaws." It was the first Jennings recording that featured the heavy, rolling beat and up-front drums that would characterize his later releases.

The album cover showed Waylon in black gunfighter's garb, standing on the sidewalk in an Old West setting. It was not a concept album (it included Buck Owen's "Under Your Spell Again," for example), but it marked the first use of the word "outlaw" in connection with the music of any prominent country artist of the day.

An important press milestone for the entire "outlaw movement was an article by Dave Hickey in the January, 1974, *Country Music* magazine. Titled "In Defense of the Telecaster Cowboy Outlaws," it was one of the first pieces to explore the impact that Waylon, Willie Nelson, Tompall Glaser, Billy Joe Shaver, Kris Kristofferson, and other "underground country" artists were making.

The article documented an "appreciation" show that Neil Reshen arranged at the Sheraton Hotel in Nashville in the fall of 1973. The show received all the more attention because it was held as an alternative to the annual country music Disk Jockey Convention. Hickey began his prophetic article with the words "Just a note to tell you I've seen the end of the beginning.

". . . [A]ll our favorite low riders, lonesome pickers and Telecaster Cowboys have been herded together, penned up and branded with a lot of dumb names like 'Underground Country,' and 'Progressive Country' and 'Hipbillies'!"

After naming the above artists, as well as Lee Clayton, Mickey Newbury, and "everybody else in town without a swimming pool!" Hickey says: "[T]he only thing most of these guys have in common is that they were born west of the Mississippi and often forget to go weak at the knees at the mention of Jeff Davis."

Hickey and a few friends who were attending the "conventional" DJ convention left that scene and drove to the Sheraton, where Waylon, Willie, Sammi Smith, Troy Seals, and others were giving their own show. "Neil Reshen . . . had done a publicity overkill and had attracted about 6,000 people to a room that accommodated 2,500 . . . ," he reported.

Let's take a closer look at Tompall Glaser and Willie Nelson, the two figures aside from Waylon Jennings who were prime forces in the early outlaw movement.

TOMPALL AND THE GLASER BROTHERS

Tompall Glaser and his brothers never enjoyed the

star status that Waylon and Willie went on to achieve, but Tompall's encouragement, example, and business savvy proved to Waylon that you *can* make it outside of the conventional system, on your own terms.

Tompall, Chuck, and Jim Glaser were born on a ranch in Spalding, Nebraska, to parents who loved country music. The brothers formed a band in the early 1950s and played local clubs, eventually gaining a short-lived series on KHAS-TV in Hastings, Nebraska.

After winning the Arthur Godfrey Talent Show and national attention, they moved to Nashville in 1958, and soon toured with Marty Robbins's road show.

They signed with Decca Records, but in its infinite wisdom the label chose to record them as a folk act— even though they continued to play country music on stage. The Glasers weren't happy.

"When I got to Nashville," Tompall said, "everything was sewed up by a few people and I didn't like the idea . . . . What I really resented were those in power not allowing things to be done any way but theirs. Working away from that was . . . like any other liberation movement" (*Popular Music in Society*, 1977, Vol. 5, No. 5).

The Glasers' first Decca LP, *This Land,* was pure folk music. They joined the Opry in 1962, and after that their career took a more country direction. They went on the road with Johnny Cash, gaining a wider audience through playing Las Vegas, Carnegie Hall, and other major venues.

Tompall and the Glaser Brothers signed with MGM Records in 1966 and began a recording career that was noteworthy, though it spawned no blockbuster hits. From 1966 to 1973 on MGM they had no smashes, but nine of their fifteen singles charted in the twenties or better, including 1969's "California Girl" (number eleven) and 1971's "Rings" (number seven). More stylists than superstars, the brothers developed warm, tight vocal harmonies and a flair for getting the most out of a melody that remains unmatched in country music.

They kept abreast of the latest pop and country songwriting trends, too, recording material from a variety of sources and eventually creating their own music publishing firm, Glaser Publications, in 1962, a daring move at that time (it's commonplace among acts in all forms of music today).

Along the way the act picked up a CMA award for Vocal Group of the Year award (1974), and were voted Vocal Group of the Decade by *Record World* magazine (1974). Tompall wrote "Streets of Baltimore," which was a hit for Bobby Bare, and the Glasers had successful records with "Put Another Log on the Fire" and "California Girl."

The Glaser Brothers split up in 1973, after fifteen years of singing and performing together. They had a successful recording studio, their publishing company counted "Gentle on My Mind" among its hit copyrights, and Chuck even had success running what became the official "outlaw" booking agency, Nova.

By the early 1970s, after having lived with—and fought—the Nashville music establishment for more than a decade, Tompall had things pretty well figured out. He had seen country music suffer with the explosion of rock in the mid-1960s, and knew it had to expand its power base if it were going to survive, let alone thrive.

He had discovered through personal experience with Decca that the trick to getting your way with a record label was to have your own *organization*. "When independent production got into it, it allowed me to form my own company and incorporate it. Then I represented a company, so when I called a record company and said I was from Glaser Productions, I was the president, and I could talk to the president, but I could talk to nothing before that as an artist" (Bane).

Tompall and the Glaser Brothers operated out of an office/studio complex at 916 19th Avenue South (where they still maintain offices), just two blocks away from the power stations of Music Row's executives.

Dubbed Hillbilly Central, the Glasers' operation was open seven days a week, twenty-four hours a day, catering to the songwriters, dreamers, and cowboys who just couldn't become part of the existing Nashville System. Among the people who made Hillbilly Central their hangout at various times were Waylon, Willie, Shel Silverstein, Jack Clement, Billy Joe Shaver, Alex Harvey, Guy Clark, Dr. Hook and the Medicine Show, Kris Kristofferson, and others.

The Glasers' studio was no hayseed operation. They may have run it more casually than RCA ran its studio, but the Glasers had all the state-of-the-art gizmos it took to get the best sound. The biggest difference was that they encouraged an artist to take time and experiment to get the best sound, while most other studios made you feel like you were fighting a stopwatch.

Tompall and Waylon were tight friends in 1973 when they co-produced Waylon's *Honky Tonk Heroes* album, which spawned the top-ten single "You Ask Me To." (The Glasers, like many other country acts, first met Waylon when he was a DJ in Phoenix.) Waylon was enjoying his new-found autonomy,

107

which Neil Reshen had helped him win from RCA—Waylon reportedly booked the first "Honky Tonk" session on the spur of the moment after a late-night pinball session with Tompall.

In the March, 1975, *Country Song Roundup* Waylon credited Tompall with helping him develop the right attitude toward dealing with record labels and the music business: "I'm enjoying the business end of the music field for the first time. I have it where I can oversee everything and I'm in control of my business and myself.

"I make mistakes, but I'm having a good time and enjoying playing music more than I ever have in my whole life. I have a great group and a great bunch of people working with me. Tompall has helped me so much by just being a friend. He's a great artist and a great person."

The Glaser Brothers regrouped from 1981–82 on Elektra Records, and their debut single, 1981's "Lovin' Her Was Easier (Than Anything I'll Ever Do Again)," earned their highest chart ranking, reaching number two. It also earned them *Billboard* magazine's Artist Resurgence Award for 1981. But their reprise was brief, and they parted ways again after only a handful of singles.

To this day the brothers are popular in Great Britain, Germany, Holland, and other European countries. Jim Glaser, against all odds and at a time when the record charts were under increasing control by major labels, made his way to the top ten and then even number one with records in 1983–85 as a solo artist.

Chuck, who suffered a stroke after the breakup, has recovered well, though he still suffers from some paralysis. He is involved in a number of music-related ventures, including the production of the

"Rocky Mountain Inn" country music TV series for Canada which he and his partner Johnna Yurcic, Waylon's former road manager, are also marketing to other countries.

Tompall released the album *Charlie*, and was of course one of the four artists on the tremendously successful *Outlaws* album in 1976. In 1977 he changed labels, to ABC-Dot, and released the album *Tompall and His Outlaw Band*. He still records, though whether his new tracks will ever be released is anybody's guess.

One of Tompall's biggest achievements was being living proof that there was an alternative, that it wasn't crazy to think that an artist ought to have a much greater amount of creative control than was commonly allowed in Nashville in the early 1970s.

WILLIE NELSON

Willie Nelson and Waylon Jennings became the most visible and successful members of the "outlaw" movement. Where Waylon tended to recede from the limelight, Willie flashed a million-dollar smile and jumped right in. He quickly initiated a July 4th Texas music festival, penned still more hit songs, and began what continues today as a persistent assault on the pop and country charts, via solo hits such as "On the Road Again" and "Always on My Mind" and many duets (such as "To All the Girls I've Loved Before," with Julio Iglesias.)

Willie Nelson was born in 1933 in the depth of the Depression in a spot on the map called Abbott, Texas (population 375), a fifteen-minute drive north of Waco in the East Texas cotton country. Willie's father was a mechanic who traveled a lot; they say Willie's mother left home one day to find work and never came back.

Raised by grandparents and various aunts, Willie got his first and last guitar lesson from his grandfather at age six. At age ten he played his first dancehall with a band that also included his sister Bobbie on piano (she's still a member of Willie's band).

In the following years Willie worked as a janitor and plumber's helper, gave guitar lessons, taught Sunday school, sold bibles and vacuum cleaners door to door, attended school briefly (as a business major at Baylor University), served in the Air Force, married, fathered — and fought a lot.

In the mid-1950s Willie took up work as a DJ, spinning records from Texas to the state of Washington. Moving back to Texas, he married for the first time, to sixteen-year-old Martha Mathews, a waitress. He moved to Fort Worth and began to develop the earnest, real-life sound that would stay by him in future years.

Nelson was a twenty-six-year-old part-time DJ who hung around Fort Worth's Jackson Highway — the redneck answer to Sunset Boulevard — when he wrote "Night Life" in 1959. He played in clubs where they strung chicken wire between the act and the crowd so the performers wouldn't get hit by flying beer bottles.

In 1961 Willie sold "Night Life" to three Houston businessmen for $150. He bought an old Buick convertible and headed for Nashville, intending to become a country music star. Instead he got a job playing bass for Ray Price.

Willie wrote songs at an amazing pace, though, and a high percentage of them were smashes. Patsy Cline hit with Willie's "Crazy" in 1961, and Faron Young's career got a great boost from Willie's "Four Walls." Singer/guitarist Claude Gray enjoyed a smash with another tune Willie sold "for a song,"

"Family Bible." "Funny How Time Slips Away," which Willie also wrote in 1961, has since been recorded by scores of artists.

These and other songs brought in hefty royalties for Willie, who lost no time in throwing the money away with both hands. He was still playing bass for Ray Price when "Hello Walls" hit. Ray and the rest of the band rode the bus to concert gigs — Willie flew in ahead of them and rented penthouses and hotel suites.

Willie Nelson, like Waylon Jennings, moved to Nashville in the midst of a marriage that was in serious trouble. Willie's second marriage, to Shirley Collie, lasted a number of years, but was a tempestuous union.

Around 1961 Willie signed with RCA, the label that would later sign fellow Texan Waylon Jennings, but he hit against the wall of the Nashville Sound that would also suffocate Waylon's early sound. "We were out on the streets trying to make it against these people who were all in offices. They'd stay in their offices all day expecting people to call 'em up and tell 'em what was going on in the music world" (*New York Times Magazine*, March 26, 1978).

Willie was a flop as an RCA artist. His records were overproduced and unfocused. He quickly charted a top-ten single — 1962's "Touch Me" — but it would be another thirteen years before he had his next hit. Willie felt RCA didn't seriously consider him as a singer. They complained that his lyrics were too "deep," that he sang funny, and that he ought to try singing *on* the beat instead of introducing a jazz influence by singing around it.

By the late 1960s Willie still wasn't selling records. After Willie's Nashville house burned to the ground in 1969, he wrote "What Can You Do to Me Now?"

and then he and his road family made Austin their base (Willie's sister Bobbie lived there). From then on they were on the road constantly. Like Waylon, Willie in 1969 found himself hitting an emotional low. That year he lost his house, wrecked four cars, and went through a divorce.

In 1970 Willie and company recorded a landmark album in Nashville, *Yesterday's Wine*. It was Nashville's first concept album—but with respect to sales it was an utter flop. After having recorded about eighteen albums Willie called it a day with RCA and took to the road, honing his sound in bars and honky tonks all over the South and Southwest.

In 1961 Willie attracted the attention of legendary Atlantic Records producer Jerry Wexler, who had produced hits by the Drifters, Ray Charles, and Aretha Franklin, who by the way recorded "Night Life." Nelson and Wexler collaborated on *Shotgun Willie*, a rough-edged, vital LP that was recorded in two days. In six months it outsold all of Willie's Nashville albums combined. In April 1972 Willie signed a management agreement with Neil Reshen, who negotiated away from RCA-Nashville some tracks that became Willie's second Atlantic album, *Phases and Stages*. That album sold 400,000 copies, and in 1973 Willie found himself becoming hot property.

In 1972 Willie married for the third time, to his current wife, Connie. Since then, though he had been known to dally with drink and drugs, he has coped amazingly well with the demands of a superstar's life. He lopes from movie set to TV talk show to concert stage and newspaper interview with an open, genial air, maintaining a positive outlook on life and an eternal interest in The Song.

"Going back to Texas has sure been good for Willie

Nelson," Dave Hickey said in the January, 1974, *Country Music* magazine. "You get the impression that when he was living in Nashville he was sending out his songs like a stranded man sends out messages in bottles, and that when he moved to Austin, he suddenly discovered that all those bottles had floated to shore among friends."

Through the years, despite all his travails as an artist, Willie has had astounding success as a songwriter, penning a slew of hits, including the above songs and "Funny How Time Slips Away," "Pretty Paper," and many others.

Willie, like Waylon, was only too happy to let Reshen harass the record labels and to structure deals that would let Nelson make music when, where, and how he thought best.

Willie's first July 4th festival was at Dripping Springs near Austin in 1972. It was not a commercial success, but he held the event "almost annually" after that, and has built it into a very popular event.

After the 1972 Dripping Springs festival, Willie hosted a major music event at Austin's Armadillo World Headquarters, which proved to him once and for all that there was a whole new audience out there waiting for his music. He phoned Waylon and said, 'Hey, hoss, I think I've found something." What Willie had discovered was that there was a massive audience of young people who were digging his music.

Waylon recalls that he went to Austin and "walked in there and saw all these long-haired kids and I thought, 'What's that crazy sonovabitch done to me now?'

"I said, 'Goddamn, Willie!' and he said, 'Just trust me. If they don't go for it, you're going down with me.' But anyway, I saw them, just like an ocean of kids, man, who freaked plum out over our music, and I couldn't believe it" (Bane).

Willie and Waylon realized they had found people who liked their music, accepted their "images," and didn't care what Nashville had to say about it.

Waylon's first teaming with Willie Nelson on an album was 1974's *This Time*, a soft, textured Jennings LP that featured Willie's backup singing, guitar playing, co-production, and songwriting (he contributed four songs to the project).

In the mid- and late-1970s, Waylon Jennings and Willie Nelson made such an impact on the country music scene that they became linked in the minds of fans to the degree that many thought Waylon and Willie were exclusively a duet act.

Waylon and Willie were selling records, but they were also making a statement with their music. They were proving that they were capable of selecting and producing their own music, and of taking a significant role in making decisions pertaining to their own careers. What really struck home with the industry was when Waylon and Willie showed that record sales could benefit from such power being put in the hands of the artist.

Chapter Ten

"The Old Guard Don't Have Control Any More"

Having gained the freedom to do their music their way, Waylon Jennings and Willie Nelson almost single-handedly revitalized country music, drawing the attention of America's huge urban audience in the process.

They had to be outlaws—if that's what you want to call them—because Nashville's System refused to treat them like the serious recording artists they were. When the System doesn't work for you, you either give in to it, or you go outside it and make up a System that works for you. Waylon and Willie opted for the latter.

Writer Dave Hickey explained how he suddenly realized "why two gentle people like Willie and Waylon would be considered outlaws in Nashville" when he described in the January 1974 *Country Music* magazine how he felt attending a party with the "accepted" country crowd of the day:

"There were a couple of [recording] artists there at the party, in loafers and pull-over sweaters, smiling the way you do when your deaf aunt is lecturing you on world affairs. The moment it was polite we excused ourselves, feeling genuine respect for the host and hostess and wishing to God we had had our teeth capped."

In the fall of 1974 Waylon was to sing his recent number one "Ramblin' Man" on the CMA Awards show. He walked out after the show's executive producer, Joe Cates, insisted that Jennings could only sing half the song. "I guess it looks like I'm a trouble-maker, but really, I want to get along with people, and have things run smooth," Waylon told the October 26, 1974, *Record World.*

"I left it because I thought it would make for a better show. I thought they expressed an attitude that did not show respect for me as an individual or for country music. I felt I had to take a stand. I really hated to leave and do all that, but I couldn't let them walk over me."

For Waylon this incident must have evoked memories of his early days in Nashville, when he and other artists were forever told where to stand and what to sing. Waylon was nominated for the Country Music Association's 1974 Male Vocalist of the Year, but he didn't win the award.

The August 16, 1974, *Newsweek* referred to Waylon as part of country music's "outlaw breed," and cited Waylon's recent appearance at New York's Bottom Line rock club.

By 1975 Waylon and Willie were finally earning recognition from the country establishment — Waylon won the Country Music Association award that year for Male Vocalist of the Year, the only CMA award he has not shared with another artist. He attended the awards ceremony — something he wasn't to do again until 1984 — because he believed Jessi would win an award for the tremendous success of "I'm Not

Lisa" (she didn't, though she was nominated in four categories).

Waylon felt uncomfortable attending the CMA awards show. He didn't like the idea of stars and friends competing. He also resented the fact that the CMA then did little to help new artists, the ones he said needed recognition and encouragement the most.

One of the things Waylon and others witnessed at that show was a reportedly drunk Charlie Rich burning the card that named John Denver the CMA's Entertainer of the Year. Ironically, there had been a protest from some quarters the year before when Rich himself had received the top CMA award, and Olivia Newton-John had won Female Vocalist of the Year. Rich's act was a vivid representation of the bitterness that many country music artists held (and many still hold) toward artists who achieve success in both the country and pop music worlds.

In early 1975 Waylon appeared on TV talk shows hosted by Dinah Shore, Merv Griffin, and Mike Douglas. He endured the customary silly banter, even acting polite when Zsa Zsa Gabor babbled away.

Waylon was hot, and getting hotter. In 1975 his *Dreaming My Dreams* album made the top fifty on pop charts, and he was earning $50,000 a month in concerts.

Willie was hot, too. Now on Columbia, he cut the album *Red Headed Stranger*, which was promoted out of CBS's Nashville office. Neil Reshen and Waylon were the first to bring Willie's album to CBS. They were so excited by Willie's tracks that they played them for a top Columbia executive—who was not impressed. He thought it sounded like a nice "demo." Disgusted, Jennings and Reshen stomped out of his office.

117

Red Headed Stranger did nothing less than boost the visibility of country music around the world with its hit single "Blue Eyes Crying in the Rain," which won Willie a Grammy in 1976. Willie had seven albums on *Billboard*'s charts at one point in 1976.

Jerry Bradley, son of legendary Nashville producer Owen Bradley, took over the reins at RCA-Nashville from Chet Atkins around 1973. A good ol' boy who had the confidence of the Nashville artist roster, Jerry also impressed RCA's New York hierarchy with his business savvy. Aware that experimentation had been going on at the Glasers' studio, and hearing that Waylon and Willie were working together on some tracks, Bradley decided to capitalize on the issue, and in mid-1975 came up with a concept that would link a group of existing tracks that RCA had on Waylon, Willie, and Jessi Colter (Chet and Waylon had produced her *Country Star Is Born* LP in 1969). Add tracks from Tompall Glaser and you have *Wanted! The Outlaws*, which was released in January 1976.

Ironically, Jessi and Willie had each outscored Waylon on the charts then. Jessi had just had a number-one country and number-four pop smash with "I'm Not Lisa," and Willie had broken through to stardom with his *Red Headed Stranger* album and "Blue Eyes Crying in the Rain." Tompall's recording career was cold at the time.

Bradley and RCA wisely saw this as a prime opportunity to raise Waylon's visibility and sales to their fullest potential, so the *Outlaws* album cover featured Waylon's photo above those of the other three artists. The album cover featured sepia portraits of the four artists, arranged to resemble a wanted poster from the Old West, reinforcing Waylon's and Willie's images as Nashville's most famous renegades.

Wanted! The Outlaws put outlaw music on the map. It was a musical summit meeting of the primary forces in a new wave of country music. The project required the juggling of the artists' timetables, and the cooperation of four major record companies (Columbia, RCA, MGM, and Capitol) to pull it off, but they did it.

The primary strength of the *Outlaws* album was that it spotlighted a movement in country music that had gone unrecognized by major labels to that point. The album was a brilliant marketing ploy, because it came on like a fresh product with all the earmarks of a musical milestone, while in fact eight of the eleven *Outlaws* tracks had been previously released. The tracks were culled from the vaults of three record labels, overdubbed, and released. The album included two songs each by Waylon, Willie, Tompall, and Jessi, plus a Waylon and Jessi duet, and two Waylon and Willie duets.

Before the year was out, *Wanted! The Outlaws* became the first platinum (one million units sold) album recorded in and promoted from Nashville. It went number-one country and hit the top twenty on *Billboard* magazine's pop LP list.

The album paved the way for Waylon's greatest successes as a recording artist — but it also stuck him with an image that he spent years trying to fight.

The most famous hit single pulled from the *Outlaws* album was "Good Hearted Woman," a Waylon and Willie duet. Five years previously Waylon had written the chorus and one verse to the song, but couldn't finish it, so over a poker game he asked Willie to help him with it when Nelson was in Nashville and staying at Waylon's house.

"I spent the night at Waylon's house," Willie told

the *Canton Repository* (February 12, 1978), ". . . and I woke up the next morning writing this song. Jessi said I wrote it on orange juice. I told Waylon about it at the breakfast table, so we finished it after breakfast."

Waylon had a number-three single with "Good Hearted Woman" in 1972, and had in the can a live version of the song from a 1974 performance in Austin. According to Reshen, Waylon took his 1972 studio version, added crowd noise, mixed his own voice down in parts, and dubbed in Willie's to make the version that became a hit in early 1976. Reshen managed both Waylon and Willie at the time, so there was no trouble straightening things out with RCA and Columbia, the artists' respective record labels.

In the fall of 1976 there was even a brief outlaw tour, including Waylon, Willie, Tompall, Jessi, and songwriter Steve Young, who had written "Honky Tonk Heroes."

In the September 7, 1975, *Houston Chronicle* Waylon spoke about the growing "outlaw music" trend: "Y'see, our music signifies freedom . . . That scares the CMA [Country Music Association] and the whole industry there. . . . I have al the respect in the world for the old style of music. But the old guard, the old legends that had control, don't have control any more. Everything's in a little bit of limbo."

Waylon liked the idea of succeeding on his own terms. But from the start the "outlaw" label rubbed him the wrong way. It didn't seem to bother Willie, and Tompall was getting the publicity he wanted. Waylon was irked by the way Tompall seemingly lapped up the publicity generated by the outlaw image: "I never did call myself no outlaw," Waylon

From left, Waylon Jennings, Tommy Allsup, and Buddy Holly, in concert at Eau Claire, Wisconsin, about a week before Holly's fatal plane crash, which occurred on February 3, 1959. Photo credit: Don Larson

WAYLON JENNINGS, left, and Tommy Allsup at the Eau Claire concert. Photo credit: Don Larson

A lean and hungry 28-year-old Waylon Jennings in 1966, shortly after being signed by RCA Records.

An uneasy-looking Waylon Jennings, far right, poses with his booking agent, Lucky Moeller, second from right, backstage at a 1968 concert in Louisville sponsored by the Philip Morris company. Also shown are an unidentified Philip Morris official, far left, Lucky's son Larry, and the Philip Morris Boy. Photo credit: Lin Caufield Photographers.

Waylon's Music Row office building. Photo credit: Albert Cunniff

Photo-poster display in Waylon's museum showing rare photos of Waylon, Buddy Holly and Richie Valens on tour in late 1958-early 1959. Photo credit: Albert Cunniff

The Outlaws Celebrate: Celebrating the success of 1976's "Wanted! The Outlaws," the first million-selling album out of Nashville, are, from left, Tompall Glaser, Waylon Jennings, Ken Glancy of RCA Records-New York, Jessi Colter, and Willie Nelson. Photo credit: *Nashville Banner*

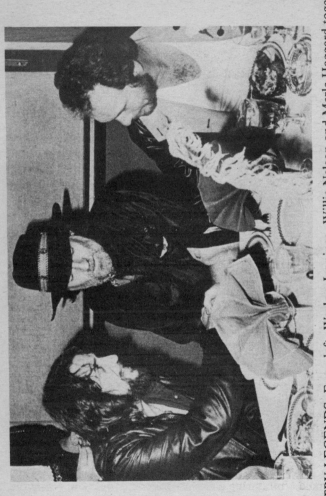

COUNTRY LEGENDS: From left, Waylon Jennings, Willie Nelson and Merle Haggard together at a Nashville awards dinner in 1981. Photo credit: *Nashville Banner*

(NS5-May 38) — WANTS HIS MUSIC TO BE HIS LEG-
ACY — "Outlaw" country music star Waylon Jennings has
his hands full during a recent television taping in Nashville
as he plucks a mandolin while his famous leather-trimmed
guitar hangs below. Jennings says he would like his legacy
to be his music, and not his rowdy image. (AP LA-
SERPHOTO) (mah 20500stf/Mark Humphrey) 1984.
SLUG: JENNINGS. Photo credit: Wide World Photos

(NY46) NEW YORK, FEB. 8 – FRIENDSHIP CAKE –
Country music stars Jonny Cash, left, and Waylon Jennings show off the cake they received to mark 20 years of
friendship in New York Friday. The musicians are appearing together at Radio City Music Hall. (AP LA-
SERPHOTO) (rwc62100stf/Ron Frehm) 1985. Photo
credit: Wide World Photos

Waylon's museum, which opened in 1984 above the Country Music Wax Museum on Music Row in Nashville. Photo credit: Albert Cunniff

Waylon's gold record collection, as shown inside his Waylon's Private Collection museum on Music Row in Nashville. Photo credit: Albert Cunniff

A burned-out looking Waylon Jennings in 1978 RCA promotional photo.

SHARP SHOOTER: Jessi Colter and husband Waylon Jennings show off their new son, Waylon Albright "Shooter" Jennings, born May 19, 1979 in Nashville. Photo credit: *Nashville Banner*

James Garner, Jessi Colter and Waylon Jennings during shooting of Waylon's 1980 TV special in Phoenix.

Waylon, Jessi and 2½-year-old Shooter relax in early 1982. At the time Waylon was finally climbing out of financial trouble, but was still two years away from kicking his 21-year drug habit. Photo credit: *Nashville Banner*

Waylon and Shooter in "disguise" as ordinary tourists in 1983.

Waylon and Jessi at home in Nashville, fall 1984. Photo credit: Steve Harbison/Photo Fair Inc.

The Metamorphosis of WAYLON JENNINGS. Photo credits: *Nashville Banner*

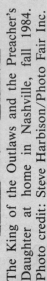

A happy Waylon Jennings today. Drug-free and financially secure, Waylon's having the time of his life.

The King of the Outlaws and the Preacher's Daughter at home in Nashville, fall 1984. Photo credit: Steve Harbison/Photo Fair Inc.

said (Bane). "Tompall once made up a bunch of things like pamphlets making people honorary Outlaws, which made me automatically sick. I said, 'That's stupid, man. You're taking the publicity too seriously. Play your music and forget that.' "

"It's a great compliment when they drop the labels off of you," Waylon told *Country Song Roundup* (March 1975). "Labels are just to tell people where you're at, and if they can't listen to you and know where you're at, then you're in trouble anyway . . .

"Some people say [my music's] not country. Some people say I'm trying to be a pop singer. If I'd wanted to cut a pop record, I could have recorded a Buddy Holly song anytime in the past five years and had a pop hit, but I didn't."

Waylon's career continued to gain momentum. The year 1976 brought the platinum *Outlaws* and other Jennings albums, and considerable exposure to the pop audience, through articles in such major newspapers as Chicago's *Sun-Times* and the *Washington Star*. The press gave Waylon glowing concert reviews—most of the time. One said Waylon "came on with the force of a brewing summer storm." Funny—a few days later a different reviewer was struck this way: "He slouches over the microphone, leers at the audience, and seldom smiles. If he were better looking, he might pull it off. But the long, greasy hair could use a shampoo. . . . He also fires visual darts if a member of his backup band dares try to upstage him" (*Daily Oklahoman*, February 15, 1976).

These remarks typify the up and down quality of Waylon's shows over most of his career. Drugs and exhaustion kept him from performing at his best in many shows, but when Waylon was "on," there were few who could top him.

On the strength of the *Outlaws* album Waylon

cleaned up at the 1976 CMA awards, receiving the top awards for Single of the Year ("Good Hearted Woman," with Willie), Best Vocal Duo (with Willie) and Album of the Year (*Outlaws*). Waylon boycotted the show, but Willie, wearing sneakers, jeans, a flannel shirt, and a bandana, bounced up on stage to accept for himself and Jennings.

On June 18, 1976, Waylon and Jessi quietly slipped down to the small town of Mer Rouge, Louisiana, to attend the marriage of Hank Williams, Jr. to his wife Becky.

In December 1976 Waylon was again flexing his muscles with RCA, as he and Reshen were involved in more contract negotiations. Waylon, who had had his hair cut and his beard shaved, joked with the audience at a Minneapolis concert: "The reason I got a haircut is I get to meet with RCA tomorrow and I want to look like John Denver and David Bowie. They [RCA] have been giving them all the money" (*Minneapolis Star*, December 3, 1976).

Tompall Glaser and Waylon had begun to get on each other's nerves, and the success of the *Outlaws* album drove a wedge between them. It all stemmed back to April 1973, when Tompall, Waylon, and Jessi reached an agreement whereby Tompall reportedly purchased a forty-percent interest in forty-six songs of Waylon's and Jessi's, as well as the rights to other songs written during the period of partnership. Tompall claimed the total number of songs he should have owned a piece of was about a hundred. The December 22, 1976, Nashville *Tennessean* published a story in which Tompall claimed he had not received the money he was owed.

After the success of *Outlaws*, which included several of these songs, the outlaws began squabbling over the loot. Tompall asked the courts for $300,000 in damages from Waylon. (Waylon eventually settled — see next chapter). Even while he was engaged in the 1976 legal battle with Waylon, Tompall said, "When the [Glaser Brothers] group broke up, I needed a brother and I went with Waylon. We're fighting now and I don't know if we'll stay together, but that doesn't matter. We did a little thing together. We're both individuals and it works out this way.

"Waylon and I together had twice the strength that we had as individuals. Maybe twenty times. People who wouldn't listen to him before suddenly listened to me. He could back it up legally. He had an ally" (Bane).

Waylon left the Glasers' Hillbilly Central in 1976 and got his own building, his current site at 1117 17th Avenue South.

Waylon was in incredible demand. No fewer than *five* Waylon Jennings albums were released in 1976: *Wanted! The Outlaws, MacIntosh and T.J., Are You Ready for the Country, The Dark Side of Fame* and *Waylon — Live*.

MacIntosh and T.J. was Roy Rogers's first feature film in ten years. Waylon sang four songs (none of them was new) on the soundtrack album, and the Waylors added a few instrumentals. Neither the movie nor the album was anything to write home about.

After the release of the *Outlaws* album, Waylon traveled to Los Angeles to record *Are You Ready for the Country*, his first album in more than a year to contain new material. Waylon's most rock-inspired album up to that time, the project was recorded at Hollywood's Sound Lab, and included a rousing cover of the Neil Young title song, and an unnecessary remake of "MacArthur Park." Also featured was Waylon's second recorded tribute to the late Buddy

Holly, "Old Friend," though the song doesn't refer to Buddy by name. (Waylon's first Holly tribute had been 1961's "The Stage"). Critics called *Are You Ready for the Country* a strong though uneven work. It entered the pop album charts alongside hot releases by Rod Stewart and Alice Cooper.

Waylon — Live released in December 1976 while *Outlaws* reached platinum certification, had actually been recorded at several concerts in 1974 in Texas. Waylon produced the project with Ray Pennington. Among this strong album's highlights are "Bob Wills Is Still the King" and "Good Hearted Woman." The latter song was making its third appearance on a Waylon LP, the previous two including Waylon's duet with Willie on the *Outlaws* album and 1972's *Good Hearted Woman* album.

Regardless of their feelings about the outlaw label, Waylon and Willie continued to record together and ride the crest of the wave. Willie's influence was felt in 1977's *Ol' Waylon* album, produced by Chips Moman in Nashville, which included their duet performance on the hit single "Luckenbach, Texas (Back to the Basics of Love)," which reached number one on the country chart and number twenty-five on the pop chart. *Time* magazine chose the album as one of the best country releases of the year, and it went on to sell more than a million copies.

The tiny hamlet of Luckenbach, Texas, a one-hour drive north of Austin, will never be the same because of Waylon and Willie's song. In mid-1977, when the town's official population was three, newspapers reported that hordes of tourists were braving dusty Texas back roads to descend on Luckenbach, which wasn't even on the map (you still won't find it in your Rand-McNally).

In March 1977 Waylon got the news that his 1975

album *Dreaming My Dreams* had been certified gold, for sales in excess of 500,000 copies. Before the year was out he also got gold albums for 1976's *Are You Ready for the Country* and *Waylon—Live*.

In 1977, Waylon and Richie Albright remixed some of Willie's old tracks for an RCA repackage titled *Willie, Before His Time*. Waylon went behind the recording console again to produce his buddy Hank Williams Jr.'s *New South* album for Warner Bros., and was soon pleased to collect another platinum disc, for *Ol' Waylon*.

Record companies couldn't put out enough product featuring Waylon Jennings. Between 1976 and 1978, eleven albums featuring Waylon's music were issued, including the albums noted above and two Cash albums, *I Would Like to See You Again* and *Greatest Hits Volume Three*.

An estimated 60,000 people flooded the Tulsa Expo Center Speedway on July 4, 1977, to hear Waylon, Willie, and a few other "outlaws" perform. Two weeks later Waylon's show alone drew 10,000 to a show to Minneapolis's Metropolitan Sports Center.

Waylon and Willie lived up to their outlaw image when they boycotted the 1977 CMA awards show. Willie had accepted Waylon's awards when Jennings boycotted the 1976 show, but by 1977 he was even joining Waylon in attempting to have their names removed from the awards balloting (they were not successful in this effort). Waylon and Willie said they were friends, and simply preferred not to be placed in competition. Ironically, that year the two were not in competition for any award.

In early 1978 RCA released *Waylon & Willie*, an album that sold extremely well, and contained the smash singles "Wurlitzer Prize" and "Mammas Don't Let Your Babies Grow Up to Be Cowboys." Nevertheless, some critics were already growing tired of hearing about pickup trucks, half-warm beer, and your warm and tender body close to mine, and referred to a "formula" that was getting old.

RCA executive Jerry Bradley conceived of *Waylon & Willie* as a natural followup to the success of the *Outlaws* package. He figured that, as with the 1976 album, he'd have Waylon overdub his voice on some of Willie's tracks, and vice versa. Bradley had an artist mock up the album cover, and surprised Waylon with it during a meeting at RCA's offices. Waylon immediately took a liking to the project, but after a few attempts at overdubbing, Waylon, Willie, and Bradley agreed that the album ought to consist of newly recorded duets.

Waylon and Willie's different reactions to the success of their outlaw music and image was highlighted at an RCA press reception at the Rainbow Room in Manhattan in early 1978 to promote *Waylon & Willie*. Willie had just completed his *Stardust* album with Booker T. Jones, and Waylon had finished his part on a concept album recorded in London.

At the reception Willie fielded questions from a slew of persistent reporters and flashed his smile for photographers. Waylon fretted, fidgeted, and withdrew into a corner, though he did reluctantly give an interview to Jane Pauley for the "Today Show." Both artists felt misled by RCA; they had understood that this was to be a quiet, intimate affair.

Waylon & Willie hit number three on country album charts in its second week of release in February 1978 and went gold less than a month after its release. It quickly shot toward the million-unit sales mark. On the strength of the album, Waylon and Willie picked up a Grammy in early 1979. They toured together for a brief time as well.

The concept album Waylon had worked on in London was *White Mansions*. Conceived by English songwriter Paul Kennerley (now known for his work with Emmylou Harris), the song cycle dealt with Georgia during the Civil War, and featured such artist as Eric Clapton, ex-Eagle Bernie Leadon, Jessi Colter, and others. Waylon traveled to Atlanta in June of 1978 to promote the album, though label restrictions kept his name from the album credits. Ironically, *White Mansions* was on A&M, the label that had reluctantly released Waylon so he could sign with RCA in 1965.

Even when Waylon and Willie performed together in concert during the height of the outlaw craze, they did not structure their show as a duet. As one critic noted, "The actual duet singing, when it did come, was by no means the high point of the night, and its brevity was undoubtedly because both men know their limitations together. Their duet singing is really more valuable as a symbol than as a tangible musicality" (*New York Times*, April 24, 1978).

In 1978 Waylon signed a new RCA contract that reportedly gave him one of the record industry's highest royalty rates at that time. RCA was moving an incredible amount of Jennings product. The *Outlaws* album was well beyond platinum (a million units sold) and still selling briskly, and his recently released *I've Always Been Crazy* album had enough advance orders to ship gold (500,000 units).

Waylon and Willie were nominated in 1978 for more CMA awards, and again stayed away from the show. Strangely, they didn't win in any category, despite the recent astounding success of the *Waylon & Willie* album, Nelson's *Stardust* LP, and the artists' hit singles, apart and as a duet.

Though Waylon and Willie are forever linked as a

musical team in the minds of thousands of country music fans, in fact they have played surprisingly few concerts together since they first shared a stage in the mid-1970s.

"Between 1978 and 1983 there were only about a dozen Waylon and Willie shows that I know of," said a former Waylon road-crew member. "But during the time I was with Waylon, there wasn't one date when someone didn't come up to me and ask, 'Where's Willie?' "

In September 1978, Waylon, ever unpredictable, made his first appearance in years on the stage of the Grand Ole Opry. He sang with an old friend Johnny Cash on "The Greatest Cowboy of Them All," a track that they had recorded in the same session that yielded "There Ain't No Good Chain Gang," but which their labels to this day have never reached an agreement on releasing.

Despite a general downtrend in record buying, in 1979 Waylon's *Greatest Hits* album rocketed to platinum status. It has since sold more than four million copies.

Waylon and Willie continued to assault country music charts in 1982, when they released a duet version of "Just to Satisfy You," which Waylon and Don Bowman had written about eighteen years before in Phoenix, and which Waylon and Bobby Bare had previously released. In 1982 Willie was also riding high on the charts with "Always on My Mind."

Over the years, especially around the late 1970s, Waylon had his spats with Willie, too, though nothing serious or enduring, just tiffs over musical direction or image. Today Waylon remains close to Willie, though Nelson, with his outgoing personality and natural ability with the press and public, has stayed on the charts and in the public eye. Waylon said of

Willie, "We're brothers from somewhere, and we're together, right or wrong, to the end, and ain't nobody gonna separate us" (Bane).

As the 1970s drew to a close, Waylon grew increasingly uncomfortable with the outlaw label. He regularly complained to the press about the label, and how it focused on his "image" more than his music.

"I'd just like to be thought of as a person, y'know, 'cause that's all I am . . . ," he told the *Houston Post* (January 19, 1979). "[T]hat picture of me as a guy who goes into a bar, sits down with his back to the wall, knocks a woman down and then tries to punch out the bartender or something like that — well, it ain't me, that's all!"

"People always go into that macho stuff when they write about me. They make it sound like my main interest in life is tearing things apart. They forget I'm a musician. That's all I've ever been" (*Pittsburgh Press*, December 1979).

More recently Jessi spoke on the outlaw image with the *Pittsburgh Press* (February 11, 1982), "That all came out of Tompall Glaser's idea and the record *Wanted! The Outlaws*. Waylon didn't even like the idea of the outlaw label then. The record sold good, so the outlaw thing was commercialism at its boldest.

"Record marketing people are always looking for a hook. Trouble is that this one grew into a brand that's just about impossible to erase. All kinds of stories and rumors sprang from that outlaw stuff. Waylon's no outlaw, never was. He's a sensitive artist.

"An outlaw is somebody who's destructive. He isn't. He's creative."

Occasional concert reviews prior to this time noted that Waylon had performed with a "sore throat" or that he "suffered from laryngitis." It is quite possible that whatever chronic throat problem Waylon had may have been made worse by his use of cocaine. In any case, while Waylon's use of cocaine increased, the reports of missed concerts and on-stage throat problems increased. In February 1977 Waylon "fought a cold" during a show in Tulsa; that August he had a "bad throat" at a Dallas show. He battled laryngitis during shows in Miami and St. Petersburg that September. These were just a few of the many signs of health problems that would be mentioned in press references for years to come.

The hard-fought freedom that they were awarded helped Waylon and Willie's music. Willie got his personal act together over the years in a way he could handle, but offstage Waylon's life was in a tailspin. Willie went onward and upward, while Waylon broke with many of his old "outlaw" friends and retreated into his world of recording studios, concerts, and drugs.

Chapter Eleven

"This Outlaw Bit's Done Got Out of Hand"

It's a warm night in August 1977 and Waylon Jennings is in a Music Row recording studio producing Hank Williams Jr.'s *New South* album. During the session Waylon's secretary Lori Evans walks in, carrying a package that Mark Rothbaum has had an out-of-town courier service deliver to Nashville.

A few minutes after Evans walks in, federal, state, and city drug officials who had been waiting outside enter the studio and arrest Evans and Jennings. The package that Evans had brought in contained cocaine.

The song that Hank Jr. and Waylon were working on at the time was "Storms Never Last."

By the end of the 1960s Waylon had been through three broken marriages, hospitalization for hepatitis, almost ten years of drug abuse, exhaustion from a frenetic road life, near bankruptcy more than once, and the disillusionment that resulted from fighting the Nashville System.

Willie Nelson's life had known similar troubles, but he took a different path after reaching the level of superstardom. Willie smiled and smiled and became an international film, TV, and concert celebrity, and socked a good bit of his hefty income into investments.

Waylon frowned, withdrew from the limelight, deepened his dependence on cocaine, and quietly slipped into debt.

Waylon rarely discusses his previous marriages, but in an interview in 1974's *Popular Music and Society* (No. 3) he said: ". . . I've been married more than most family men . . . . [W]hich is worse, one bad marriage or four bad marriages, which is it? I mean, they're all bad. It can seem like the worst thing in the world if it's your problem."

In 1977 Peter Guralnick, author of *Lost Highway*, noted, "The Waylon Jennings image today is one of almost unrelieved gloom. Pain seems to gnaw at him like a vulture, and even his music seems bruised and weary."

Much of Waylon's trouble stemmed from his abuse of drugs — and that stemmed back many years. Waylon's first experience with pills came in February 1959, while finishing up the Winter Dance Party tour after Holly was killed. It's not clear whether he continued taking pills after that, but he had certainly picked the habit up in Phoenix by 1962 when he was performing regularly in clubs. He has openly referred to his drug use in numerous interviews.

Waylon was already well into the pill habit by 1969, as he admitted to John Grissim: "Now I do believe that the line of work we are all in requires us to give the folks in there [the audience] everything we've got. And of course a lot of fellows who pick and sing pretty near every night have been know to use pills to help them overcome the natural fatigue which one encounters on the road . . .

"As for myself, I have been known on occasion to indulge in such things — from time to time, I mean . . . Chet Atkins thinks it's a sin to even look at one" (Grissim).

After mentioning a few artists whose lives and careers had been destroyed by drugs, Waylon laughed in his talk with Grissim, then said, "Yeah, give 'em [pills] a chance and they'll do you in."

Waylon's drug problem worsened around 1971 when he began taking cocaine. He was remarkably candid about his drug use in the December 9–23, 1971, *Door*. Asked whether he takes pills, Waylon replied: "Yeah, I take pills. Uppers. I can't get anything out of smoking [pot]. I sit and grin and that's about all. I go to sleep and put everyone to sleep around me."

Over the next twelve years Waylon's drug use would grow to where it became life-threatening. He said numerous times in interviews — *Newsweek* (August 26, 1974), *Plain Dealer* (July 23, 1978), etc. — over those years that he had quit drugs cold, but he was only fooling himself.

Waylon was hospitalized around early 1972 with hepatitis, and his addiction to drugs hampered his recovery. In his hospital bed Waylon looked at his problems, and decided that his life was going down the tubes because of too many days on the road, too many people pushing him too hard, too much drug-taking, and too much self-pity.

Waylon was supposedly the model for Rip Torn's near-psychotic country music star in 1973's critically acclaimed film *Payday*. Torn played a singer hooked on amphetamines and whiskey, who partied his way through the seedy world of all-night bars, motel rooms, and smoke-filled backstage dressing rooms.

Waylon says his friend Shel Silverstein was hired as

a consultant for the film to insure that it captured Waylon's character. Jennings said Torn even copied an eye problem he had at the time—one of Waylon's eyes was terribly bloodshot and hurt constantly. "It had come to the point when I couldn't talk to people, I couldn't sing, I couldn't do anything—I thought—unless I was high . . . I'd lost all confidence. In my singing and everything" (*Houston Chronicle*, September 7, 1975).

"I was very lonely for a long time. Yeah, I was really into a self-destruction thing. I *thought* I was havin' a good time, but there was a lot of self-pity in there, too. That's all depression is, I think—the highest form of self-pity . . ." (*Photoplay*, February 1975).

Waylon apparently was also hospitalized in Texas during the summer of 1977 for treatment of his drug addiction. John Young, a doctor friend in Texas who said he "helped" Waylon out during this time, lost his license in 1980 and was sent to jail because he continued to liberally prescribe pills for Waylon and others.

In the June 10, 1980, Austin *American-Statesman*, Young said he helped "get Waylon off everything he was on" by admitting him to an Athens, Texas, hospital for six weeks. Young admitted writing prescriptions for hundreds of uppers for Jennings.

The Dallas *Times-Herald* noted that at Waylon's mid-August 1977 show in that city, "Without a doubt, Waylon Jennings was in no shape to perform . . . . Looking haggard and dispirited, the famous Nashville outlaw did his best to get through the night, stretching painfully to reach old familiar notes and avoiding others altogether . . .

"It was . . . discouraging to see him so debilitated in a summer when he has reportedly spent some amount of time in a hospital kicking a drug habit. One had hoped to hear and see him revitalized."

The front page of the August 24, 1977, *Nashville Banner*—the same issue that announced Waylon and Willie's planned boycott of the upcoming CMA awards show—featured the news that Waylon and two of his associates had been arrested the night before on drug charges "after allegedly receiving a drug shipment from New York."

The arrest was made after a probe by federal narcotic agents in New York and Nashville, and agents of the Tennessee Bureau of Criminal Identification and the Nashville U.S. Attorney's office.

Charges against Waylon were eventually dropped, but more because of apparent mishandling of the case by federal narcotic agents than anything else. Waylon was fortunate, and well represented—he used more than four lawyers to defend himself.

A courier service in New York had become suspicious about a package they were asked to deliver to Waylon in Nashville. Mark Rothbaum, then an aide to Waylon's manager Neil Reshen (and today one of Waylon's booking agents), had arranged for the package to be delivered by the courier service. He had aroused their suspicion when he made several anxious phone calls to the service from Nashville, inquiring as to the package's whereabouts and giving conflicting reports on what it contained.

Rothbaum reportedly first said the package contained "very important contracts," but in a later call said it held "very important music recordings." The courier service grew suspicious (they only ship documents) because of Rothbaum's manner and, as is their right within the law, opened the package. Inside they found a number of bags of a powder that they strongly suspected was an illegal drug.

Drug Enforcement Administration officials called in on the case confirmed that the powder was cocaine. They determined that the package held about twenty-seven grams (one gram shy of an ounce), representing a Nashville street value of about $3,000. Agents confiscated all but about two grams of the drug. The New York drug officials re-wrapped the package and placed it aboard a flight to Nashville, phoning ahead to alert Nashville Tennessee Bureau of Criminal Identification agents. Officers from both agencies tailed Waylon's secretary, Lori Evans (who had been sent to pick up the package), from the airport back to the American Sound studio, where Waylon and Hank Williams Jr. were at work.

What did the agents do wrong, then? They waited outside the studio for five to ten minutes. Having left so little cocaine in the package and having waited so long before entering the studio, when they finally charged inside, they failed to retrieve the two grams they were trailing. After a four-hour search, all the investigators found were traces of cocaine on two wet plastic bags found near the toilet.

Jennings and Evans were arrested, and Rothbaum later faced charges as well. Waylon and Lori were charged with conspiracy and possession of cocaine with intent to distribute, were fingerprinted and photographed, and released on their own recognizance. They faced a maximum sentence of fifteen years and $15,000 in fines.

Twelve hours after appearing in federal court on drug charges, Waylon was on stage, receiving standing ovations from 9,000 people who packed Nashville's Municipal Auditorium to watch him sing with fellow "outlaw" Willie Nelson.

Later, in the tense scene where newsmen were jockeying to get film and photos of Waylon walking in and out of federal court, a WTVF-Nashville TV cameraman was struck in the face by a soft-drink can reportedly hurled at him by Waylon's friend Richie Albright. Richie was later bound over to the Grand Jury and charged with aggravated assault.

Charges against Jennings and Evans were eventually dropped, but drug officers were not about to let the case go. The August 26 *Nashville Banner* reported that Mark Rothbaum, then twenty-eight, had surrendered to federal officials in Connecticut (Reshen's office was in Danbury) and volunteered to come to Nashville to face charges in the cocaine matter.

Charges against Rothbaum were dismissed "without prejudice" on October 4, 1977, which meant the government was still free to indict either Rothbaum or Jennings at a future date. Sure enough, Rothbaum was indicted on charges of distributing cocaine in early 1978, and pleaded guilty on April 24 in U.S. District Court in Bridgeport, Connecticut, to a single count of distributing cocaine. Lori Evans was granted immunity from prosecution in exchange for her testimony on the case. All of this was reported by the press.

As if all that weren't enough, around this time another member of the Jennings family got into trouble because of drugs. Waylon's daughter, Julie Jennings, then nineteen, was arrested in Nashville along with two other people following an alleged drug buy. A police raid netted eleven pounds of marijuana.

Waylon's drug bust cropped up in his autobiographical 1978 album *I've Always Been Crazy*, which includes the track "Don't You Think This Outlaw

Bit's Done Got Out of Hand." "Yeah, that song is absolutely true," Waylon said (*Houston Post*, January 19, 1979). "We were overdubbing something on a Hank Williams Jr. session when it happened. They charged me with cocaine possession, and I didn't possess any, so they dropped the charges on me.

"Seems like the police would realize that the dealers of the stuff are *not* the hillbillies, y'know? They arrested me on charges of 'distributing,' which is just crazy! Making the kind of money I make, why in the hell would I want to be in the cocaine distributing business? And so, right after it happened, I got the title for that song."

For whatever reason, the album *I've Always Been Crazy* is a solid Jennings release, one that features Waylon's voice at its strongest, matched against the Waylors at their best in great song after song. Also included are a Buddy Holly medley, and solid interpretations of Johnny Cash's "I Walk the Line" and Merle Haggard's classic "Tonight the Bottle Let Me Down." The LP touched on Waylon's feelings toward the press, his image, and his career. It debuted in *Billboard* at number twelve, and shipped gold. Waylon remarked that he considered it one of the two best albums of his career, alongside 1975's *Dreaming My Dreams*.

Before 1978 was over, Waylon learned that *Waylon & Willie* had topped the million-unit sales mark.

The year 1979 brought more legal trouble to Jennings, this time regarding former outlaw buddy Tompall Glaser. According to Glaser, in April 1973 he paid Waylon and Jessi $10,000 for a forty percent interest in Baron Music, including forty-six songs written by Waylon and Jessi as well as interest in songs composed from that point on. By 1976 Tompall said he owned part of one hundred tunes through this deal.

By January 1977, after the *Outlaws* album was an established smash, Tompall was unhappy with Waylon and Jessi's handling of the agreement, and he filed suit against them for what he considered his share of the royalties. Because the songs involved included "I'm Not Lisa," "Good Hearted Woman," "Are You Sure Hank Done It This Way," and others, and because royalties included income from the hugely successful *Outlaws* album, Tompall expected a good deal of money.

The July 6, 1979, *Tennessean* reported on Glaser's claim that Waylon and Jessi refused to pay him what they owed him, even after an arbitration panel had decided that Tompall was owed $160,000. Now Tompall was seeking the original $160,000 plus $160,000 in damages.

According to Tommy Jennings, who had run Baron Music for Waylon before Tompall bought into the business, Waylon eventually forked over the amount he was told to pay, and bought Tompall out of Baron Music. Waylon later sold the company to the Welk Music Group. (Today his publishing company is Waylon Jennings Music.)

Reeling from his drug use, legal battles, road exhaustion, and money troubles, Waylon turned in increasingly spotty performances on record and stage.

Prior to *I've Always Been Crazy*, Waylon had released a string of albums that, sales aside, had frequently met with less than enthusiastic critical comment. *Are You Ready for the Country* (1976) had seemed weak, lacking the fire and inventiveness of his previous releases. *Ol' Waylon* (1977), despite its sales success, had seemed to some fans and critics like a regression to 1972, with Waylon working his way unenthusiastically through other people's hits. *Waylon & Willie* (1978) included mostly bland reworks of others' material, though the remake of Ed Bruce's "Mammas Don't Let Your Babies Grow Up to Be Cowboys" came off quite well. The 1979 *Greatest Hits* album recapped Waylon's top tracks from the past decade.

Waylon's laryngitis cropped up again at a concert in Salt Lake City in September 1979. In early November of that year, in El Paso, he had trouble with his guitar, amp, memory, and balance on stage at the University of Texas, quipping to the crowd, "I'm doing the best I can. I didn't say I was smart. I just said I'd show up." Waylon eventually cranked up and gave a great finish to that show.

In March 1980 Waylon was met with—you guessed it—another lawsuit. This one came from old friend and occasional co-producer Chips Moman, who, by the way, was the owner of the studio where Waylon was arrested in the 1977 drug bust. Chips was suing Waylon and RCA Records, claiming they had failed to give him proper credit or pay him royalties he believed he was due from several of Waylon's records.

Chips said he had been unable to get a full accounting of sales to determine whether he had been getting the two percent of gross sales which he claimed he was owed. He also said that he had not received credit for producing such Jennings hits as "Luchenback, Texas," "The Wurlitzer Prize" and "Mammas Don't Let Your Babies Grow Up to be Cowboys."

That wound was obviously healed, for Chips continues to produce some of Waylon's music today.

An even bigger legal mess cropped up later that year, when Waylon became involved in a controversy relating to a lease he held and then dropped on the

American Sound studio. In June 1980 Waylon asked the Davidson County Chancery Court to define his responsibilities to the studio. He alleged that the owner, Alan Cartee (Chips sold the studio to Cartee), had failed to maintain the studio properly, and he sued Cartee for about $150,000 for problems that cropped up during recordings that he said stemmed from the studio's faulty equipment.

Waylon originally leased the studio on October 25, 1978, for one year at a rate of about $17,000 a month. He extended that lease in 1979, but then suddenly moved out in the middle of the night in May 1980. Cartee brought suit against Jennings for $750,000, alleging that Waylon had taken about $40,000 worth of recording equipment from the studio that belonged to Cartee, had caused considerable damage to the premises, and had left owing almost $100,000 on his lease.

The suit dragged on and continued to pop up in local papers through July 1981. Waylon claimed financial damage because tracks he cut at the "poorly maintained" studio could not be released. A recording engineer who worked at the studio testified that Waylon's marathon recording sessions damaged the equipment, and that Waylon and his crew used drugs to "stay up for three or four days" for sessions (*Tennessean*, July 15, 1981).

That wasn't all. Cartee filed for protection from his creditors under Chapter 11 of the Federal Bankruptcy Act, and blamed Jennings for his money troubles. Cartee said he was forced to sell American Sound at a substantial loss after Waylon abandoned his lease.

Jennings dropped his suit against Cartee on July 15, but couldn't resist responding in print to Cartee's claim that Jennings was the main cause of his bankruptcy. Waylon told WLAC-Nashville radio newsman Eddie Parker that he thought Cartee's deposition "was pretty funny—I kind of like fiction."

The July 16, 1981, *Nashville Banner* revealed Waylon crying the "Sue Me, Sue You" blues: "I think my own mother might sue me next, probably for being sued so many times." Richie Albright added, "It's gotten to where if someone says, 'We'll sue you,' we say, 'Fine. Get in line.'"

On July 17, 1981, the Cartee-Jennings matter came to an end, with Jennings being ordered to pay only about $60,000 to Cartee—less than a tenth of what Cartee had sought in his suit. The judge ruled that Jennings did indeed breach his contract at the studio, but that by music business standards he had not done it maliciously.

Waylon was involved in at least one other lawsuit in the 1980–81 period. This class action was filed by an irate fan who was disgusted with the quality of Waylon's performance when he walked off the stage forty minutes into his show on June 8 in Duluth, Minnesota, complaining of a sore throat from laryngitis.

Legal problems can be settled; Waylon's drug problem did not go away so easily. In fact, his drug addiction was the major problem that beset him after his other personal, label, and legal problems had cleared up as he moved into the 1980s. It was not until 1984 that Waylon would really get a handle on his addiction, once again with the help of his closest friends, Jessi Colter and Johnny Cash.

"This business can be like a merry-go-round or a roller coaster. And for anyone who comes from a background like mine, it just takes you a long time to catch up and get any kind of hold on what's happening to you. It takes a long time to bring it all together—and I'll admit that for quite a few years, I didn't. It had hold of me!

"I shrank back from fame. I never had any kind of goal to be Number One or anything like that. I never really thought about bein' famous. And when it finally happened to me, it caught me by surprise. I didn't understand a lot of it, and the truth is I was scared by it all.

"I just wanted to play my music and I really didn't give a shit about all the rest of it" (*Country Rhythms*, March 1985).

Chapter Twelve

Black on Black

In mid-1978 the Waylon Jennings/Johnny Cash duet "There Ain't No Good Chain Gang" hit number two on the nation's country charts. Waylon said he played the song that eventually became the flip side, "I Wish I Was Crazy Again," over the phone to Cash in 1976 when Cash was in Hamburg, Germany, and that the two decided to cut it and "Chain Gang" at the 1976 session. Waylon appeared that May on Cash's "Spring Fever" TV special.

(In August 1978, Cash and Jennings again went into the recording studio, this time to record a Cash composition, "The Greatest Cowboy of Them All" and "Even Cowgirls Get the Blues." To date CBS and RCA have not reached an agreement that would allow release of these tracks.)

The CBS-TV series "Dukes of Hazzard" premiered in January 1979, featuring Waylon as The Storyteller and starring John Schneider (himself a fine country singer) and Tom Wopat. Waylon had done the soundtrack music and narration for a 1975 movie called *Moonrunners*, loosely based on the B-movie saga *Thunder Road*. Waylon and steel guitarist Mooney contributed fourteen songs to the movie; no soundtrack album was released. The people behind *Moonrunners* had a concept for a TV show roughly based on that movie's idea, and they approached Waylon about doing a "Dukes" pilot.

Jennings and his band wrote and performed the "Dukes" music on the road, without seeing the shows! Waylon filled in between scenes with homilies and observations on the action, never appearing on camera, though his hands are seen playing guitar in the show's introduction. The producer sent Waylon scripts and he recorded his narration on the road, either in his bus or at a radio station along the way.

The producer sent Waylon film clips, too, but he rarely looked at them, preferring to ad-lib when the mood struck him. In fact, one scene had to be re-shot because Waylon took liberties with the script. "They give me all the freedom in the world. I like that," he said (*Minneapolis Star*, June 6, 1980). Waylon wrote the "Dukes" theme song before he ever saw the show, after receiving basic guidelines from the show's production staff.

Jennings said he was happy to stay off-camera in the background, though the show's producers repeatedly tried to get him to go before the camera, even for a walk-on part. "I don't want a lot of things that come with being a recognized star. I like to run loose, just go out and play pinball or whatever." (He relented in 1984 and took a featured role in one episode.)

Said he liked doing "Dukes" for one reason: "Kids love it. I have a lot of fun with it, and I aim my narration towards kids." His son, Shooter, especially liked the General Lee car Waylon had from the show. Waylon said Shooter's favorite character was the curvy Daisy Lee.

In 1979 Waylon also appeared on TV specials

hosted by Johnny Cash ("Spring Special") and Cheryl Ladd ("Charlie's Angel Goes Country"). His single "Amanda" went number one country, as part of an incredible hot streak that Waylon enjoyed from 1974–80, during which time twelve of his eighteen RCA singles went number one (including two duets with Willie Nelson).

Reports circulated in April 1979 that Waylon had accepted a role in an upcoming film to be titled *Urban Cowboy*. He initially accepted but later refused a role, saying the producers had signed too many artists to appear in the picture to suit him. (At the same time, Willie Nelson was preparing for his film *Honeysuckle Rose*.)

By early 1979 Waylon had won his musical freedom, and found acceptance with resulting product — seven gold albums, three platinum albums. He was making (and spending) a lot of money. He had married a wonderful woman, and he had every reason to be happy. But he often felt miserable, and wondered if he'd ever see the end of his drug and money troubles.

If you can point to a single event in Waylon's recent life that seems to have helped put him on the road toward controlling his drug and money problems, it has to be the birth of his and Jessi's son, Waylon Albright "Shooter" Jennings, on May 18, 1979. Waylon looked forward to being a father again: "I'm going to try to follow it all the way through. I was so young when the other kids were born, I didn't even know what was going on. I want to be around this time when we're raising it — plan the tour carefully" (*Los Angeles Times*, November 18, 1978).

The name Albright is for Richie Albright, Waylon's bosom buddy and drummer since the mid-1960s in Phoenix. The initials W. A. carry on a Jennings family tradition. "We nicknamed him Shooter because his daddy's such a pistol," Jennings told an audience at his San Diego concert.

Waylon commented proudly on his son in concerts and in print, boasting during a Salt Lake City show in early September 1979: "He looks so much like me you wouldn't think Jessi had anything to do with it." After coaxing Shooter out on stage to wave to the audience, Waylon told the audience at a January 1984 Merrillville, Indiana, show: "He's like me, kinda shy. He looks so much like me when he was born that he didn't know for sure who the mother was."

Waylon had risen above being hotly against the outlaw label by 1979: "What it amounts to is that I have to have a person to relate to in corporations. . . . At RCA I trust Jerry Bradley [then head of the Nashville division], and he has done a lot for me. The album covers are all his ideas. He has come up with some great ideas. Jerry and I didn't agree for a long time. But even then, he respected me and I respected him. He knows exactly what I am about musically" (*Country Music People*, May 1979).

"I think the worst mistake anybody can ever make is to deal with a corporation or a government organization on a personal basis, a man-to-man basis. There is nothing human about corporations. They're just structures made up of a lot of people who know what their jobs are but don't know nothin' else. . . . And no one can make a decision. Corporations are like a chain-link fence—one guy passes a problem along to the next, who sends it along to the next. My advice is, don't do battle with them on their

147

terms on their ground at their time" (*Penthouse*, September 1981).

In terms of controlling his career, Waylon never had it better; despite all his record success, financially he never had it worse. His *Greatest Hits* album sold at an incredible pace (it has now sold more than four million units), other albums had strong sales, and Waylon was in constant demand for concerts — but money was going out faster than it was coming in.

Late 1979 brought Waylon's *What Goes Around Comes Around* album. A "different" LP, mellower than any previous Waylon release, it quickly went gold and spawned the number one ballad "Come With Me." Critics noted that it contained interesting tracks (such as Rodney Crowell's rocker "Ain't Livin' Long Like This") but that it wasn't Waylon's most captivating performance.

While Waylon maintained a vigorous schedule of recording and touring, critics began to question the creativity and energy level of his recordings. His perennial drug/exhaustion/throat problem cropped up regularly: In February 1980 Waylon had canceled a show in Jackson, Tennessee, because of laryngitis . . . in June 1980 he walked off the stage before a packed Duluth (Minnesota) Arena forty minutes into his show because he had a sore throat.

Waylon's enduring respect for his first producer/mentor brought him before the TV camera in 1980 to be interviewed briefly on the PBS-TV "Reminiscing" special on Buddy Holly.

Jennings then released a string of albums that sold well, but many fans and critics shared the opinion that the energy level on the LPs was "dangerously low." Waylon would later admit this was not his most creative period.

Music Man (1980) was a commercial success, but as one critic wrote, "Hearing Waylon's continual cowboy cutup for an entire side isn't funny. It's enough, already" (*Tulsa Daily World*, May 30, 1980). Though the album contained the title gem, Waylon's cover of the Kenny Rogers hit, and the hit "Theme From the Dukes of Hazzard," it was apparent that Jennings's good-ol'-boy song formula was losing its appeal with critics. Noel Coppage wrote, ". . . it wouldn't be ideal as your *first* Waylon album; as an umpteenth one, it works fine . . ." (*Stereo Review*, October 1980).

In 1981 Waylon's *Leather and Lace* duet LP with Jessi quickly went gold, and included two singles that were fairly well received, "Storms Never Last," which reached number seventeen, and "Wild Side of Life," which hit number ten.

An avid sports enthusiast, Waylon in February 1980 sponsored the car of his friend, attorney, and CPA, Gary Baker, in the Daytona 500 (Baker is also co-owner of the Nashville Speedway). "I like the motors and the way they have to drive—slide around the curves. That knocks me out. The noise goes up your backbone. That's what music does" (*Minneapolis Star*, June 6, 1980).

Two months later Jennings performed in a benefit concert for Jimmy Carter's re-election bid. The *Washington Post* (April 24) reported that "Waylon's entourage are the only people at the reception wearing black T-shirts which read, 'Support Your Local Hell's Angels.' . . . [Waylon] follows Mrs. Carter to the reception line, walking as if he's poking one shoulder at a time through beaded curtains; and he puffs on a cigarette he hides inside his hand, street-corner style."

* * *

In late July 1980 Jennings returned to Phoenix, where almost twenty years before he had established the sound that would lead to his RCA signing. On Waylon's previous appearances in Phoenix, his ex-wife Lynne had sent a sheriff to visit Waylon and discuss back alimony. Apparently this matter was settled by the time of this TV special.

Waylon wanted to come back to Phoenix to show his musical roots. J.D.'s and Wild Bill's clubs didn't exist any more, so he chose Mr. Lucky's, which was owned by Waylon's old friend Bob Sikora, who as a club manager had signed many checks for Jennings back in the 1960s. (J.D.'s changed its name to the Whiskey River club, which was gutted by fire in the early 1980s.)

Jennings was to perform at Mr. Lucky's nightclub as part of an ABC-TV special, "Waylon, Starring Waylon Jennings." "In one night, more people will see him than bought his records in twenty years," boasted Jack Thompson, the show's co-producer (*Arizona Republic*, July 30, 1980).

James Garner, who was then between TV roles, co-starred in the special, along with Jessi Colter. A feisty character himself, Garner had walked out on the "Rockford Files," and had not yet begun work on a short-lived revival of "Maverick." He had also walked out on "Maverick" in 1960, during a contract dispute with Warner Bros.

They shot footage at Mr. Lucky's and in concert at the beautiful Red Rocks Amphitheater outside Denver, also showing Waylon's two buses and forty-foot trailer traveling on the road.

Phoenix welcomed Jennings with open arms. A club veteran who remembered Waylon from his days in the early 1960s told the July 31 *Phoenix Gazette*

150

that Jennings was a "great human being who came from the street, paid his dues, picked cotton as a child. One day he decided to make music and he's been doing that for the past thirty years—his way."

Waylon performed at Mr. Lucky's before a capacity crowd of about 700. Virtually no "regular locals" got inside for the taping, though as many as 2,000 people waited in line for hours outside the club! The only ones ushered inside were invited guests. As the producers wanted footage showing an overflow crowd, they let the people outside simmer in line from the hot afternoon into the evening. Things got so bad, in fact, that ABC handed out free passes for another night, and Waylon later promised to play again for pass-holders on his next visit to town.

Just because Waylon decided to do a little TV, that didn't mean he was going to open up entirely. He refused to allow ABC photographers on the set, and wouldn't talk to ABC-TV publicists or out-of-town journalists. During the taping at Mr. Lucky's, Waylon sang "Waltz Across Texas" a second time when the cameras didn't get everything they needed during the first run. When asked to sing it a third time he grumbled, "I don't know it three times."

Also included in the show was an after-hours pool match between Jennings and Garner, a self-confessed Waylon Jennings fan. At the Red Rocks show, Garner walked on-stage before 12,000 people and joined Waylon and Jessi in singing "Luckenbach, Texas."

Waylon was delighted to return to Phoenix, (which still has a special place in his heart). He told the *Gazette*, "Coming to Phoenix for this concert is like coming home for me. I have a very real love for many people here. They were with me when I needed them.

"The Phoenix audiences have always been a favorite of mine, and tonight was just like it was in the past. I've always felt real good about Phoenix people and even the producers and the network people told me that they've never met a more cooperative group."

When the special aired on October 23, 1980, it received good reviews, but as one critic pointed out, "Waylon Jennings is *not* a television star. He's a country singer and that's exactly what is presented" (Bud Wilkinson, *Arizona Republic*, October 23, 1980). *Daily Variety* said it was "the kind of TV musical special that makes a person wish the set had stereo speakers—because there sure isn't much to look at, though there's plenty to listen to" (October 27, 1980). The show's producers announced at the time that they had signed a five-year deal with ABC-TV for Waylon to do additional specials, but none has materialized since then.

Waylon's next TV appearance was in the mid-1980, in the made-for-television ABC film "Oklahoma City Dolls," which also starred Susan Blakely. He played Blakely's macho boyfriend, a semipro football player who objects when she decides to start a female football team.

Jennings agreed to be the "surprise guest" at a Cowboy Roundup held to raise money to restore the Kentucky Governor's Mansion in October 1980. He had befriended the Governor and Mrs. (Phyllis George) Brown at that year's Kentucky Derby. That same month he toured in concert with Hank Williams Jr.

Waylon and Jessi traveled to the small, dusty town of Alpine in dusty southwest Texas, about thirty miles north of the Mexican border, to appear on a British TV documentary about the American cowboy in April 1981. "An outline was sent to me, and they wanted to know if I'd do the narration and be there and talk with people and do the music for it. I'll tell you how much I wanted to do it: I found out how much I was going to get paid *after* I agreed to do it! . . . What we're trying to show is what a cowboy really is. I don't think people have ever seen that. They've seen a Hollywood cowboy, but they've never seen what one is really like" (*Penthouse*, September 1981).

Waylon genuinely admires cowboys, and enjoyed taking part in the spring roundup at the 06 Ranch. During the week's filming he had a great time singing ballads of the Old West at Alpine's Crystal Bar, later joining a group of local musicians who sang and played at a local dance. (This special aired as "My Heroes Have Always Been Cowboys" on the Nashville Network cable TV in the spring of 1985.)

Waylon croaked his way through a December 1981 show in Oakland, California, though a reviewer said the concert was nevertheless "homey and warm-spirited." A photo from the *Oakland Tribune* (December 14, 1981) shows him looking washed out.

This was definitely a musical, physical, and emotional low point for Waylon. If you were to look at *Billboard* magazine's list of the top fifty country songs for 1981, you'd never know that an artist by the name Waylon Jennings existed—he didn't have a single tune on the list.

Waylon was still candid about drugs in his print interviews, though he usually implied that he had kicked drugs. "I was busted on a drug charge awhile back, and that worried me badly for one reason. . . . I worried about the influence it had on kids. I've always wanted to say, and I do want to say, that drugs are wrong, they're bad, and for kids the worst thing in the world" (*Country Music*, April 1981).

". . . I've said, and I'll say it forever, if I had my

153

life to do all over, I'd never do anything to my body that's artificial.

"You finally get to where the drugs are ruling you. . . . I think [you] gotta remember trying to help somebody in that position, the worst thing you can do is to write them off . . . and the most defensive person in the world is the person who has a problem and is trying to survive, and trying to defend himself."

Throat problems continued to plague Jennings into 1982, cropping up again at Las Vegas, where he rasped his way through a show, calling his throat problem "the creeping crud." "Sorry 'bout my voice, but don't my clothes fit me good?" he joked with the crowd.

Waylon logged another hit single with "Shine," from the soundtrack of the movie *The Pursuit of D. B. Cooper.*

Waylon's *Black on Black* album, released in early 1982, got lackluster reviews, though as with every other album Waylon had done since *Outlaws* it sold well. An observant Walter Dawson noted in the Memphis *Commercial Appeal*, "*Black on Black* . . . has a wearisome feeling. . . . For some reason, Waylon seems to be holding back or, at best, just holding on" (February 28, 1982). Even *Billboard* magazine, which almost always ran nothing but glowing reviews at that time, said *Black on Black* didn't live up to the usual Jennings standard.

The album contains solid though uninspired covers of Johnny Cash's "Folsom Prison Blues" and Hank Williams's "Honky Tonk Blues." "Women Do Know How to Carry On" picks up the pace a bit, but on balance the album rides on a middle level, occasionally dipping into the maudlin.

True to his word, Waylon made good on his promise to perform for the people who were shut out of his July 1980 show in Phoenix. He played Mr. Lucky's again in March 1982 and gave free entry to those patient souls. ABC-TV was again there, this time to tape Waylon for a segment of "20/20."

In the fall of 1982 RCA released *WWII*, a duet LP with Willie Nelson that contained six solo performances by Waylon, and five Waylon and Willie duets. A less than stellar effort, it contained the single "(Sittin' on) The Dock of the Bay," which only reached thirteen on *Billboard*'s country singles chart. Other tracks included "Mr. Shuck and Jive" and "Last Cowboy Song."

In the January 16, 1983, *Pittsburgh Press*, Waylon again spoke proudly of Shooter, then three and a half: "He can make me glad all over, and then it kinda hurts when he suddenly tells me, 'I wanna play by myself.'

"Know what? He's got a full set of real good drums we bought him, and that little fella's better at music than me, 'cause I never could play drums. He already knows syncopation. I'm soon gonna take him to the studio with me."

Waylon admitted that his preoccupation with his career kept him from being a good father to his children by prior marriages: "I was in too much of a hurry then. Out on the road . . . too busy to spend enough time with the kids."

In mid-1983 Waylon and Jerry Reed embarked on a series of concerts to benefit local charities throughout the South. The Give 'em a Hand tour was underwritten by Maxwell House Coffee.

Waylon's music seemed to take a rebound in early 1983, marked by the release of three albums, *Take It to the Limit*, a Willie Nelson LP on which Waylon appears; *Waylon and Company*, featuring Jennings along with other country stars; and Waylon's own *It's Only Rock 'n Roll.*

Take It to the Limit was marred by Chips Moman's shapeless and slick production, a sound that some say is remarkably like the production that drove Willie back to Austin to start with! But there's no denying that Moman has produced some monster hits, including such recent smashes as "Always on My Mind" and "To All the Girls I've Loved Before." Waylon and Willie sing duets on the title song, "Blackjack County Chains" and "Old Friends," while Waylon handles "Why, Baby Why" himself. The title song, an Eagles tune, reached number eight on country singles charts in late 1983.

Waylon and Company presents Waylon and nine guest singers: Hank Williams Jr., Ernest Tubb, Jerry Reed, Emmylou Harris, Willie Nelson, Tony Joe White, Jessi Colter, Mel Tillis, and even actor James Garner. Two weak singles were pulled from the album: "Hold On, I'm Comin'," with Jerry Reed, peaked at twenty, and "I May Be Used (But Baby I Ain't Used Up)," with Waylon handling the vocals alone, peaked at fourteen.

Waylon did have fun making the album, though. "On some of them it took four or five hours just to sit us down and make us stop being funny with each other," he said (*Cincinnati Enquirer*, December 10, 1983).

" 'Course you *know* I can't ever catch up with Willie in the duet department. The only one he hasn't worked with is Lassie, and I hear he's tryin' to set that one up" (*Country Song Roundup*, January 1984).

The most interesting of these three albums released in the latter part of 1983 is *It's Only Rock and Roll*, which included a song that is still Jennings's most recent number one song, "Lucille (Won't You Do Your Daddy's Will)," a slowed-down cover of the Little Richard classic. The album also contained Rodney Crowell's title song, a medley of the "outlaw" hits, and Waylon's "Living Legends (A Dying Breed)," a swipe at the hypocrisy of many of the people in Nashville's music industry, who chip away at an artist's freedom and control during his life, then revere him when he's dead.

"I put 'Living Legends' on the new album as sort of a joke. What it says is, you got to be able to laugh at yourself. You've got to be able to see the humor in things. I've done some of the dumbest things in the world. You got to be able to laugh at them" (*Dallas Times Herald*, November 13, 1983).

Chapter Thirteen

"I May Be Used (But Baby I Ain't Used Up)"

Waylon found nothing to laugh about in December 1980, when he sat across the table from one of his managers at a hastily-called meeting in Los Angeles and the man informed Waylon that he was $2 million in debt. Waylon had a choice: he could declare bankruptcy, or he could work like a dog for the next year and a half to try and break even.

Waylon had apparently not been aware of the true depth of his financial trouble until June 1980, when he was already on the verge of bankruptcy. It's not that he had stopped making money; on the contrary, his income was at an all-time high. He was earning $25,000 a night in concert, almost 200 nights a year, and his records were selling at a breakneck pace.

The problem was simple—more money was going out than was coming in. Several of Waylon's road crew, tired of working amid the paranoia, strain and confusion, and worried about hearing any day that their paychecks would bounce, deserted the sinking ship. "Before I left [along with a number of other road crew members], everything was going sour for Waylon. He saw everything going down around him," one of those who departed said.

Confused and angry, Waylon called his entire band and road crew together while in Las Vegas for a show, and said it wasn't working, and that he was thinking of quitting the business. He released all but about three of his band members and three of his road crew.

"Waylon called everyone together after one show and told us he'd had it, that he couldn't handle the drugs," one of those who left around this time said. "He said, 'Individually I love you all, but collectively you can kiss my ass. We tried to make a run of it this summer, tried to change a lot of things. But when I'm out here, I can't handle the drugs. I want to spend more time with Jessi.' "

Most everyone, including Richie Albright, left the next day. Waylon went to Malibu, California, in attempt to kick drugs, and he did go off them for a brief period. But "California isn't a real good place to get off drugs," he later told a reporter.

The strain was getting to Waylon. In June he halted a show in Duluth, Minnesota, because of laryngitis. The next month he cancelled shows at the Milwaukee Fest and Heart of Illinois fair for the same reason.

Waylon's manager, Neil Reshen, who had recently undergone heart surgery, had all but ceased his music management work. According to a close source, Waylon had come to the end of his rope with Reshen. "When you're making that much money and you're going broke, who do you point a finger at? Management," the source said.

Waylon, who was still deeply involved in drugs,

drew closer to Mark Rothbaum, who had served time in prison on the cocaine rap three years earlier. Jennings severed his ties with Reshen and put Rothbaum in an advisory/booking capacity.

He learned that somehow he'd gone through a huge advance that RCA had given him less than a year previously. "I'd gotten a $3 million advance from the record label, and that was all gone. Everything I owned was in hock . . . . A lot of it was my own fault, because if *you* don't care, then you can't expect anyone else to. I don't know if anyone actually stole from me or not. But if they did, they're the ones who are going to have to live with it."

For whatever reason, the money was gone. Waylon had nowhere to go to borrow any money—the banks and his record label had advanced him all they could. He was going broke!

In retrospect it's not hard to see where a lot of the money went—at the time, Waylon's payroll was running about $1.5 million for a twelve-month period. He carried a road crew of thirty-eight, including five drivers (for three buses and two tractor-trailers). He had ten full-time staffers at the office back in Nashville, and he had leased the American Sound studio next to the office. "He hung out there," the former road crew member said. And that's not counting all the money he threw away on cocaine.

A person who worked for Waylon at the time said, "It was just utter chaos. A lot of it I attribute to drugs, and the fact that he's always had a tendency to surround himself with ass-kissers and 'yes men'" (*Country Rhythms*, March 1985).

"We always stayed at nice hotels," another source who asked not to be identified said. "A lot of artists put their people up at one cheap hotel, while they stay in a nice hotel themselves. We always stayed at Hyatts, Hiltons—no Holiday Inns for Waylon. I think that stemmed from his younger days on the road.

"In 1978 we did a lot of dates for $17,500. In 1981 we didn't work for much less than $50,000. One weekend in Las Vegas we got $200,000." Lear jet rental fees added to his tremendous payroll crippled Waylon. It was not unusual for him to gross more than $200,000 in a week—and come out of it $30,000 in the red, after paying a $70,000 Lear jet bill and the salaries and expenses of a few dozen workers.

"When we played Vegas or Tahoe, the hotels would give us maybe fifteen rooms as part of the deal. But we'd book around twenty-six and pay the difference. Plus it seemed then that every time we were doing real good business, Waylon would get sick and miss concerts. Once he got sick and missed three gigs, and we lost $200,000.

"It was not unusual during a three-week tour for us to play only nine dates out of a possible twenty-one."

Waylon's drug problem, natural shyness, and insecurity caused him to retreat further from the scene, avoiding interviews and TV appearances, even showing up at RCA as little as possible. "I just wanted to play my music, and I didn't much give a shit about the rest of it—including the money. So I withdrew. I shrank back from it all," he said (*Genesis*, December 1984).

Waylon formed a new band and was back on the road within a few months, but things didn't get any better. In November 1980, knowing that drastic measures were needed, Waylon shut down his Nashville office and cut his staff from twelve down to two, Marylou Hyatt and a co-worker. Waylon had his office moved to the attic of Marylou's house, and operated from there for the next eight months. The band and road crew were off the payroll, but they all stayed in touch, waiting for Waylon to gear back up.

In December 1980, Marylou Hyatt gave Waylon's books a complete going-over, and was shocked at what she found. She flew out to meet with Bill Robinson (Jennings's TV agent and co-manager) and Waylon in Los Angeles. After checking Marylou's findings, Bill sat across the table from Waylon and told him he had two ways out: He could declare bankruptcy, wipe his hands of the whole mess, and start over, or, assuming he made a certain amount of money each month and handled his expenses properly, after a year and a half he might work his way back up to zero.

Waylon didn't need to deliberate; he chose the latter course. He said, "I pick that, because I'm not gonna tell anyone I owe money to that I'm not gonna pay them." A top accounting firm was brought in to help straighten things out, and Waylon Jennings began a long, hard climb back to solvency.

In January 1981 Bill Robinson decided that the quickest way for Waylon to get the most cash was to play Vegas, so he got Waylon booked there for ten days. Waylon used the money to pay his people, including back pay for the two months they had been off the payroll. This time Waylon held on to the money that was left, and established a trust account to pay the bills. Gone were the bookkeeper, assistant bookkeeper, publicist, assistant road manager, etc. Waylon had his office contact all the people he owed money to, and they soon went on a payment schedule designed to get Waylon out of debt after one and a half years.

That August, Waylon's office moved from Marylou's attic to a location in Brentwood, Tennessee, a suburb of Nashville. All this time he retained ownership of his former Music Row office building, but left it vacant. That was cheaper than operating it, as it needed new air-conditioning, carpets, and wallpapers, and Waylon had other priorities—paying off his bills. Only when he could see that things were getting close to even did Waylon have a contractor give an estimate on the required work.

The balance books were shaping up, but not Waylon. In December 1981, a reviewer wrote that Jennings sang with "a cold or a bad throat" in a concert at Sacramento, California. In February 1982 while playing Vegas, Waylon fell prey to—what else?—Las Vegas throat. The following month he experienced voice problems during a show in Phoenix. Other reports came in from other venues. "20/20" ran a segment on Waylon in the first half of 1982.

In October 1982, approximately a year and a half after Waylon had begun his new financial schedule, he made the last payment on his debts and reached "zero." Since then he has never looked back. He never missed a payment, and his credit remains great. Waylon moved back into the 17th Avenue South office, with a staff of two where there had once been as many as sixteen! The books are kept up to date, and the accounting firm sends a man out to personally look over Waylon's books, so he can red-flag a small problem months before it turns into a big problem. Waylon's net worth has doubled over the two and a half years since he worked his way back to even.

Back when Waylon's books were getting their first going-over, it was discovered that Waylon's taxes weren't being paid. Waylon had a manager, accountant, and bookkeeper, all of whom were receiving very good salaries for whatever they did — but no one paid the taxes! A person close to the scene said, "In the period 1978-1979, there were as many as sixteen people employed in the office. It was a common sight to find four or five of them sitting around playing cards all day long. But when Waylon walked in, the cards disappeared."

Waylon once had people who opened doors, and other people who closed doors, but no more. Where there were once as many as thirty-eight people on the road with Waylon and sixteen back in Nashville on the office staff, now there's a road crew of eight (paid only when there are concerts) plus the band, and an office staff of two.

Waylon's money problems are over. He never had to declare bankruptcy, and he's had to pay no tax penalties. When he was in deepest trouble Waylon was "advanced out" from everyone. It's a good idea for recording artists to operate with some advances, money that the record label (or bank) gives the artist up front and then hopes to recoup out of record sales. But Waylon was so far advanced out with every lending source that he was a liability to everyone he dealt with.

Today Waylon is breathing easy — he knows he's covered. There are persistent rumors that his money troubles stemmed from his getting ripped off, but the real problem may have been a lot of workers doing a less-than-adequate job. Nobody knew that the other guy was also doing a poor job, and as a result a lot of things just didn't get done, or were done wrong. This was true at every level of operation, in accounting, records, publishing, road reports, and on down the line.

Today Waylon has a tight, efficient management structure to guide his career. WGJ (Waylon Goddamn) Productions provides Waylon's records to RCA. Marylou Hyatt is president of WGJ. She reports to JRM (Jennings/Robinson/Margolis), Waylon's management company. Margolis's strengths are in legal matters, deal-making, and career management. Robinson is a veteran in the world of television and films, and also has a voice in career management. Waylon handles the music, and of course also takes part in the decision-making.

For the first time Waylon's finances were in order, but it still left one major problem in his life: drugs. His use of drugs stemmed back to the early 1960s in Phoenix, where he took pills to give him the energy to work days as a DJ and nights as a club singer.

Regarding his early pill-popping days in Nashville with apartment-mate Johnny Cash, Waylon said, "I don't really know where I started. Somebody said, 'Here . . . try one of these.' I told him [Cash], 'I didn't give you the first one, I won't give you the last.' Neither one of us could handle it and the other one knew it. It got to the point where it nearly killed both of us.

"I weighed 135 pounds soaking wet . . . I just got sick and worn out. I had to stop, literally, and go in the hospital" (*Tennessean*, July 9, 1983).

Waylon's drug use started with pills, but he eventually became a heavy cocaine user. A former insider with Jennings's road crew recalls that Waylon's drug problem was simple: "Toot [cocaine]. He did major amounts. One time before a big show we had five days of rehearsals. Waylon stayed up all five days!"

One of Waylon's booking agents from around this time said Jennings's use of cocaine became something of a joke. "Waylon Jennings and George

Jones—we used to call them the Powder Twins," he said.

The former road crew member who says working for Waylon was "a real fine experience" adds, "I have a lot of respect for the man [Waylon] and his music. We [the road crew] called ourselves the Waylon Machine—a real fine organization, some of the best in the business." But he also recalls the worst part of the experience: "Anyone who's involved deeply in drugs develops a paranoia—and that spread to the crew. Everyone was kind of looking over his shoulder all the time." On top of the paranoia, "Waylon's basically a pretty shy person, and it's easy for him to close in around his 'road family' and isolate himself."

"I had a really bad habit," Waylon admitted. "I was an addict. I didn't just do a little drugs—I did them constantly. My life would have been so much better and simpler for a whole lot of years if I had left them alone. But it finally got to where, due to cocaine, I had practically withdrawn from the human race.

"I'd hit bottom, my voice was shot, and I'd bottomed out as a human being. I was ready to die, really."

By the spring of 1983 Waylon's cocaine addiction had become so bad that his family and friends feared for his life. Jessi was force-feeding him high-protein milkshakes. "Jessi went through hell," he said. "She was watching me die."

Depressed, he'd wake up wide-eyed at 4 a.m. at his beautiful Brentwood home. "I'd go out and sit by the pool in the dark and think about what I was doing to me, to my people and to my family. It was ridiculous—the money I was spending on cocaine, and what it was doing to my life" (*People*, October 22, 1984).

Waylon got help from his friends Johnny Cash and Bob Sikora, owner of Mr. Lucky's in Phoenix. As he had done earlier with his financial trouble, Waylon began his most serious effort to date to kick his drug problem. Cash had recently been through treatment for chemical addiction at the Betty Ford Center in Rancho Mirage, California. Waylon's pride and fierce independence prevented him from seeking help of that kind—he had to work this out by himself.

With Sikora's help, Waylon leased a home in the Paradise Valley suburb of Phoenix and moved there with Jessi and Shooter. He took long walks in the woods, worked up the resolve to kick the cocaine habit. After a month of seclusion his health improved, and he returned to Nashville. He stopped taking drugs on March 31, 1984, and has stayed "clean" ever since.

Waylon revamped his road crew and band again, telling everyone who worked for him or wanted to be around him "that they had to drop [cocaine] or find something else to do or somewhere else to go."

In the June 15, 1984, Ottawa *Citizen* Waylon revealed, "Just recently I kicked a bad drug habit. I was on drugs for twenty-one years. I'm completely free of that and I never intend to have anything to do with it again."

The next day in the Nashville *Tennessean* he said, "I'll tell you exactly the truth. About a year ago I was bored with everything. I was on drugs so bad. I don't want to bore nobody with it, except I just want to make a statement, you know?

"And I don't mind it bein' printed. I spent twenty-one years doin' drugs and I never would do that again. They say 'never say never,' but I am sayin' NEVER.

"I didn't go to a hospital or anything. It takes a

167

brave man to do that. I did it myself. 'Course I had a lot of good, positive people around me."

Chief among those people, Waylon said, was his wife Jessi. "She really has been my strength. She's had a hard time with me, and she has lived through some rough years."

Waylon had come out of a dark, lonely tunnel. "I'm fired up about being back in the human race, I really am. And I'm happier now than I've ever been. I'm more into my music, more into my family, more into livin'.

"It's like now everything's running as smooth as clockwork."

Since kicking dope Waylon says he has found new joy in life. "I know that I can never even touch it [cocaine], and I don't want to. I'm a drug addict, and if I ever do it again I'll be right back on it . . .

"The good, real feeling of being off drugs keeps me high with my family. I can be dead tired when I come home, but if Shooter wants to play or Jessi wants to talk, I've got time and energy for it.

"It's a new high for me. I wouldn't trade this feeling for anything" (*People*, October 22, 1984).

Waylon switched booking agents a number of times between 1981 and 1983. For a short while he was booked by the Shorty Lavender Agency, and gave some management control to the high-powered, Los Angeles-based Management III, led by Jerry Weintraub. After a brief stay at the Regency Artists booking agency Waylon switched again in early 1983, to the Nashville-based Top Billing agency. Around October 1983 he made another change in his booking arrangement, splitting the responsibility for concert bookings between Buddy Lee Attractions of Nashville, and Mark Rothbaum's company in Danbury, Connecticut. Waylon's show still includes Jessi Colter and the Waylors.

Waylon played a number of dates in April 1984 with Willie, with whom he was so closely identified from the outlaw days—but with whom he has played surprisingly few concerts. In Houston, Waylon was in a good spirits on stage, mugging for the crowd, kidding around with Jessi, and changing the lyrics of his songs for humorous effect.

The spring of 1984 brought the release of *Never Could Toe the Mark*, Waylon's last album recorded while he was still on drugs. It's full of energy and "groove" songs, but is weak lyrically, and does not feature Waylon at his vocal best. "Talk Good Boogie" has a great beat, but the lyric is surfacy. "The Entertainer" is a lackluster cover of the Billy Joel hit. The title song, the album's strongest cut, reached number six as a single in the fall of 1984, while the album was floundering in the thirties on *Billboard*'s country chart.

Never Could Toe the Mark, which included four new songs written by Waylon, was "the most high energy album I've ever done," according to Jennings. "I did it especially that way as a summer album. I think in the summer people like to listen to uptempo songs.

"Me and my band really got into doing this one. I think somebody told 'em I was over the hill or something, and they decided it was up to them to try and save me" (*Country Rhythms*, March 1985).

In mid-1984 Waylon made videos of five songs from his *Never Could Toe the Mark* album, and became the first Nashville artist to be spotlighted on Cinemax cable TV's "Album Flash." In between the songs, Waylon discussed his career and personal life with a "psychiatrist" played by actor Robert Duvall, a big fan of country music. Johnny Cash and Jessi Colter also made cameo appearances in the half-hour program, which included the songs "Whatever Gets You Through the Night," "Settin' Me Up (To Put Me Down)," "If She'll Leave Her Mama," "Where Will I Be Without You," and the title track.

Waylon again reached into the rock field for song material when he chose "Settin' Me Up," a Dire Straits song that had been recorded for the country-rock style by Gail Davies, and by guitar genius Albert Lee.

The *Never Could Toe the Mark* album came out the month Waylon quit drugs (March 1984), and he owed RCA another album before the year was out, so he went into the studio and recorded an album of other people's songs. He didn't want to write songs while he was trying to put so much energy and attention into getting well. (That explains why there are no Waylon Jennings compositions on his mid-1985 album *Turn the Page*.)

Asked by the Ottawa *Citizen* (June 15, 1984) whether the "outlaws" were now part of the Establishment, Waylon replied, with none of his former bitterness about that label, "No, I don't think so. At least not consciously. I think what we have is co-existence. We're definitely more accepted than we used to be.

". . . Labels like the 'outlaws' are for merchandising and selling records. You have to have a slot to put your hits [in], but it's got nothing to do with the music."

In July of 1984 Waylon finally went before the cameras for "Dukes of Hazzard." After five years of featuring just his voice and hands on the show, and after having a hit single with the theme song, he guest-starred in an episode titled "Welcome Back Waylon Jennings," which aired that fall.

Jennings's song "People Up in Texas" was used in the movie *Moscow on the Hudson*, but Waylon wasn't happy with the tune. He said he likes to write music without seeing the video vehicle it will appear in, but in this case he saw the film first. "Consequently, after I wrote it for that, I felt detached from the song, you know?"

The year 1984 also brought the release of *Waylon Jennings' Greatest Hits, Vol. II*, which contains the "Theme From the Dukes of Hazzard," as well as a new track, "America," which turned out to be a hit. While watching the 1984 Summer Olympics on TV Waylon was inspired to write a song about America, but then remembered hearing a patriotic song on a 1973 Sammy Johns album, so he went back to record it.

"The best way to describe how I feel about America today is what's happening to the Statue of Liberty," Waylon said. "She is being repaired."

Leo Kisrow, who worked for Waylon on the road from 1978–81, said he saw Waylon at Opryland when he was taping a TV special in late 1984, and "he seemed like a whole new man. Waylon sought me out—he saw me down the hall and called out my name, asked how my wife was doing. When we worked together he was never like that. . . . The paranoia was gone, he seemed like a different person."

Larry Corbin agreed that Waylon's a new man. "The last time I saw Waylon was when he and Willie played Lubbock a few months back. Waylon looked good, and said he'd never go back on the drugs any

171

more. He looked and talked like he used to."

"I just *worked* my way out of trouble. What kept me in the business was that if I did anything else, I didn't know if I could even live. [Music] and pickin' cotton are about all I know how to do. And they got cotton-pickin' *machines* now. So I'm in trouble if I have to go back to that."

— Waylon Jennings
(*New York News*, January 8, 1984)

Chapter Fourteen

The Preacher's Daughter and the King of the Outlaws

WAYLON JENNINGS ON JESSI COLTER

"When I first met Jessi, I weighed 138 pounds, my voice was rough and I was wallowing in self-pity and depression. I was just about giving up, but she was the one who helped me through those times. Since then, it seems like every time I have a problem Jessi helps me through . . ." (*Record & Radio Mirror*, February 16, 1974).

"I had gotten to the point where I thought it would be impossible for me to be married, and I guess it still would be except for her. She was perfect for me. She put career and everything aside until I got straightened out.

". . . She believed in me when most people were telling her she was crazy to even see me" (*Los Angeles Times*, November 19, 1978).

JESSI COLTER ON WAYLON JENNINGS

"Waylon is one of the most honest, hard-working

and ethical people I've ever seen, and no egomaniac like some people in this business. He has real love for his brother, and I think he shows it more than most, well, 'straight' people do" (*Philadelphia Inquirer*, June 1, 1975).

Waylon's third marriage was on the rocks when he met Mirriam Johnson Eddy, a dazzlingly attractive brown-haired, hazel-eyed writer/singer who had recently divorced Duane Eddy after seven years of marriage . . .

"First time [I got married] I was [eighteen], and I thought she was pregnant," Waylon winced. "We got married at 3 p.m. and at 8 we found out she wasn't. My second wife was pregnant, my third wife thought she was, and my fourth wife, Jessi, is probably the greatest thing that ever lived" (*People*, September 29, 1975).

". . . I didn't really grow up until I was about twenty-five or twenty-six, I guess. I think I was an idiot until about then. 'Til I got to realizin' what was going on in the world.

". . . [W]hen I was a disc jockey . . . , I'd moved from Littlefield to Lubbock, and I was a hero in that town . . . I was married then. And women kinda like disc jockeys. I guess it's one of the fringe benefits.

"Well, I didn't do too much harm to all of 'em, I don't think. . . . I wasn't too good in them days, you know, too straight. But that was the first attention I'd ever really had, you know, that amounted to anything. It warps the mind just a little bit when the women really come on" (Grissim).

The woman we all know as Jessi Colter entered the

world as Mirriam Johnson on May 25, 1943, in Phoenix. She was the sixth of seven children born to Arnold and Helen Johnson. Arnold was an inventor/geologist/race car builder, and Helen saved souls as a Pentacostal preacher. (On Mirriam's birth certificate her father's occupation is listed as mechanic, and her mother's as housewife.) The Mesa suburb where they lived was largely Mormon, and the Johnsons were often made to feel uncomfortable because of their "different" religious beliefs.

"My mother was in the cosmetic business. Then she was in the hotel business. Then she was converted and saved at the age of twenty-seven and became a minister. And this was a day and time when women weren't allowed to do much of anything. She was quite a rebel."

When, at the age of thirty-eight, she gave birth to Mirriam, Helen was minister of the Lighthouse Mission in Mesa, Arizona. At first Mirriam traveled with her mother when Helen had revivals at various churches. Then mother got her own tent, and held her own revivals. By age eleven Mirriam was the musical director for the congregation of about a hundred, playing piano and accordion at her mother's Holy Roller crusades.

"As a child I was always in church. I grew up quite shy, pretty much of a loner, going to my piano for companionship."

"Mother would always announce me as her beautiful brown-eyed doll. My eyes were never brown — they were hazel. I had to keep telling her all my life, 'Mother, my eyes are hazel.' I played accordion until I realized my voice wasn't loud enough to sing over the accordion, so I went back to the piano" (Bane).

"I concluded at the time just what I would do . . . that I would write and sing. I knew then that I would

175

be somewhere in music. That's where I would be happiest. . . . I knew when it came to getting married or whatever, that whoever I was with would have to be centered in music. Because it was a great love of mine."

By fifteen she was performing in school assemblies and local talent shows. "I was really somethin' on the 'Lou King and the Rangers' talent show on Phoenix TV when I was in school. I did the 'St. Louis Blues'—really worked on that. And some darn accordion player won it!"

Later Mirriam landed occasional jobs singing with a western band at a Phoenix nightclub, but as the club served alcoholic drinks, she had to sneak away from home to do it.

At sixteen around 1959 she met Duane Eddy, then a well-known pop artist, who had logged such hits as "Raunchy" and "Rebel Rouser." "My sister Sharon [who later married Nashville record producer Jack Clement] . . . found out that Duane Eddy was looking for a singer to produce a record with. And she managed to set up an audition for me," Jessi explained.

Duane eventually produced a few songs on her, including "Young and Innocent," Gene Austin's "Lonesome Road," and Kitty Wells's "Making Believe," which were released on Jamie Records under the name Mirriam Johnson.

They recorded in Phoenix and Duane did some overdubbing in Los Angeles, and finally the tracks were released on Jamie Records. Eddy asked Mirriam if she'd be interested in going on the road and promoting her record and she said sure. The summer after her high school graduation they toured, playing Dick Clark's "American Bandstand," the Steel Pier in Atlantic City, and many nightclubs. Mirriam and

Duane worked with stars such as Chubby Checker, Frankie Avalon, Brenda Lee, and others.

Mirriam's records failed to attract national attention, but she fell in love with Duane Eddy in the process, and they were married in Las Vegas around February 1963. Mirriam said good-bye to her family and moved with Duane to Los Angeles, where she and Duane lived in Beverly Hills, just down the street from Robert Mitchum in Coldwater Canyon.

After her marriage, her career faded. She traveled with Duane, but not always as a performer, choosing instead to devote herself to raising their daughter, Jennifer, who was born April 5, 1964. Duane and Mirriam traveled to England, Germany, South Africa, and other spots around the world.

In Los Angeles, Jessi "was really happy, though I missed my mother and Cream of Wheat for two years. I was ready to pull out of Phoenix. And raising our child Jennifer was really a trip for me."

Among his other life and music career credits, Duane Eddy is responsible for introducing Jessi Colter to Nashville—and to Waylon Jennings.

Mirriam first met Waylon in Phoenix in 1967, while she was accompanying Duane on one of his tours. Eddy had heard that Waylon was recording, and he dropped in at the studio to pitch Waylon a few of his songs (Mirriam had some material, too). Duane brought his wife with him to a Waylon Jennings/Anita Carter recording session, at which Mirriam sang a demo of her composition "Living Proof." She was fast becoming an accomplished writer, and would soon have songs recorded by such acts as Dottie West ("No Sign of the Living"), Hank Locklin, Nancy Sinatra, and Don Gibson.

Jessi recalls her first meeting with Waylon, around 1967: "I sang with him! I had written a duet and wound up in a studio, standing on a box singing my song with HIM! I stood on a box about six inches high so that I could reach the microphone and do the tune with Waylon.

"So we were working on the demo and he just stopped the whole session, stepped back from the microphone, and said 'Goll-eee!' He just couldn't believe I could sing so loud.

"Waylon stopped the whole tape. He looks at me and says, 'Goll-eee!' The fact that I was singing so loud startled him. You see, although he has great volume and color and all, in the studio he sings very softly. So we made it through the duet and all, and I figured well, that's it. . . . But it was quite a long story from then until . . . we got married."

Eddy took Mirriam to see Waylon's show at the Phoenix nightclub J.D.'s, where Jennings had become a regional legend. Eddy admired Waylon, especially the meticulous way in which he spoke with each member of his band, letting them know how he wanted them to play on every note of every song.

"Waylon was at a club there called J.D.'s—he played there for a long time and he was setting Phoenix on fire," Jessi said. "He made it come alive like the lights go on somewhere. The cowboys would drive in hundreds of miles to see him. And the women would get dolled up from Saturday to Saturday to go see Waylon Jennings. So I just had to see what it was all about."

Around this time Duane also took Jessi on her first visit to Nashville: "I was very impressed. Harlan Howard made a deep impression. The whole spirit, the enthusiasm I saw there, as opposed to the way session musicians and artists on the Coast approached things—it was a little more dry, a little less exciting than I found it to be in Los Angeles." Duane also pitched Jessi's tapes to Chet Atkins, who headed RCA-Nashville.

"I credit Duane for introducing me to country music," Jessi said. "I had heard it and liked it, but never really identified with it. Then I went through a period when it came to express what I felt, and I came to understand it. It has a tremendous feeling I hadn't heard anywhere else, I felt at home with it and as a result, fell in love with it."

The Eddys divorced amicably in 1968 (Jessi, Waylon, and Duane are all friends today), after about seven years of marriage, and Jessi returned to Phoenix, where she began making a serious effort at writing country music, under the name Mirriam Eddy.

When her marriage to Eddy had dissolved and Waylon's third marriage (to Barbara Rood) was falling apart, Mirriam saw Waylon again in Phoenix, where she had moved to be back near her family.

She was drawn to Waylon, but had mixed feelings about the man who was so different from her. She "wrote him a letter, telling him how much I liked the new things [records] he had just done and that all the things I'd heard about him couldn't be true, because of the way he sounded — he *had* to be basically a good person. I felt like I was taking a chance, seeing him . . . but I would."

Jessi admits that Waylon did not make the best first impression on her. "I could picture orgies going on in his motel room, and I just said no way that I was going to go anywhere around him" (Bane).

"One night he was trying to get me to go home with him and he says, 'Well, look — would it help if I told you I studied for the ministry one time?' He scared me to death, but I was totally stricken. It was just the start of a great, great romance."

Waylon was genuinely impressed with Mirriam's writing and singing abilities. He published some of her songs and offered to produce her. Around the spring of 1969 he brought her to Chet Atkins (who had met her before, with Duane). Waylon and Chet co-produced Mirriam in 1969.

Mirriam had to find a name to record under. Recently divorced from Duane and not yet married to Waylon, she didn't want to be called Mirriam Eddy, and she didn't want to go back to Mirriam Johnson. Casting about for a name, she remembered stories her father had told her of a supposed "distant relative," Jesse Colter, said to have been a counterfeiter who traveled with the famous outlaw Jesse James (historical records fail to confirm this). Mirriam altered the spelling of Jesse's first name, and in the fall of 1969 "Jessi Colter" was born.

Chet said around time of signing her: "I was interested in Jessi the first time I heard her, about five or six years ago. She sounds like a female combination of Don Gibson and George Jones. . . . She's also one of the brightest, most analytical people I ever knew, and one of the most interesting women I've ever talked to."

The first Jessi Colter album, RCA's *A Country Star is Born*, was released in early 1970. Unfortunately, neither Jessi's album nor several singles which RCA released from it did a thing—they didn't even chart. (Some of the tracks were repackaged in 1976 for the *Outlaws* album.)

Jessi and Waylon were married on October 26, 1969, at Helen Johnson's church in Mesa. Jessi moved with Waylon into a Nashville villa which they dubbed Fort Apache. She soon put her career efforts on hold and put all her efforts into being Mrs. Waylon Jennings.

"See, at that time Waylon was having a lot of difficulties with his career. It was taking a good deal of his energy to do what he was trying to do. So I just my put energy behind my man and his career.

"But I kept right on writing. I must write. It's a part of me, like breathing . . ." (*Music City News*, June 1975).

Waylon's lifestyle and career problems were taking their tolls. After three marriages and five children, eight years of drug abuse, horrible money troubles, and growing dissatisfaction with the way his music was turning out at RCA, Waylon was nearing his first serious "burnout." Two years into his marriage with Jessi he hit rock-bottom when he contracted hepatitis.

"He was sick, real sick," Jessi said. "And that's when it flashed to me that all my energy needed to be—not that I had spent all that much energy on my career—but I knew then that Waylon really needed something to happen in his career." Three of Waylon's children by previous marriages had come to live with Jessi and Waylon, so Jessi aimed all her efforts at her family and marriage.

Waylon credits Jessi with being "the inspiration I needed" to give up amphetamines around this time. But he soon "graduated" to cocaine, and when his addiction became life-threatening eleven years later, Jessi went through hell "watching me die," Waylon said. Jessi force-fed Waylon a diet of milkshakes laced with honey, fruit, proteins, and vitamins.

In 1974, with Waylon's career under better control, Jessi decided to place a bit more emphasis on her career, and she signed with Capitol Records. Her first Capitol album, *I'm Jessi Colter*, issued in 1975, contained her first Capitol single, the smash "I'm Not Lisa." Ironically, with her first chart record Jessi did what Waylon has never done — she had a number-one country hit that crossed over to being a top-five pop single.

Jessi actually debuted "I'm Not Lisa" on "Hee Haw" around 1972, three years before she recorded the tune. She said that after that one syndicated broadcast many people, even young girls, came up to her on the street in cities across the country and asked about the song. "I thought it was unusual for people to remember a song that way, just from hearing it one time. So when I got ready to do some more recording again, I thought about it."

"I'm Not Lisa" is about a girl who becomes painfully aware that she is not her man's first love when her man calls her by another woman's name. Jessi says it was written from life — one night Waylon mistakenly called her by another woman's name. "I guess all women worry about the girls walking around in our men's minds. It's just our natural insecurity" (*Philadelphia Inquirer*, June 1, 1975).

"The rhythm pattern of the title line came from an old music theory exercise that I used to do . . . the whole song came to me right out of the blue." She said she had the title for three or four years before actually writing the lyric. " 'Lisa' is a very female song — little girls understand what I'm saying in that song. It's a very personal thing."

Waylon and Jessi were both hot in 1975 when they toured in concert together. They had recorded duets together before (their "Suspicious Minds" went top thirty on country charts in 1970), but now Jessi had a hit with "I'm Not Lisa," and Waylon was riding high with his hit album *Dreaming My Dreams*. They drew great crowds to Caesar's Palace in Vegas, and played before 20,000 in New Orleans's Super Dome. Waylon and Jessi also appeared together on the "Mike

Douglas Show" in 1975.

Jessi's stage show was often knocked (though somewhat gently) by critics, and she's the first to admit that her show is a bit amateurish. She says she'll never be a professional when it comes to performing live. "It's something I've got to ready myself for. I'll always have an amateur approach. I'll never look professional, because if I do, I can't stay turned on. It has to be absolutely spontaneous."

Los Angeles Times music critic Robert Hilburn, a big fan of Waylon and Jessi, gave this assessment of a Jessi Colter show: "Though her nervousness in doing what was her first concert in some four years may have made her lean too heavily on commenting on Jennings, it would probably be better in future shows to maintain a little more distance. She has the ability to stand on her own. Colter is a strikingly attractive woman with an ear for inviting melodies and lyrics that are straightforward, but exceptionally convincing" (*Los Angeles Times*, May 20, 1975).

Jessi's followup single to "Lisa" was "What's Happened to Blue Eyes," and it made it to number-four country and climbed halfway up the pop charts as the flip side of "You Ain't Never Been Loved (Like I'm Gonna Love You)," a song she wrote a few days after meeting Waylon.

Jessi Colter has written another classic country ballad—"Storms Never Last." "The songs I've written always touch Waylon," she said. "I almost threw 'Storms Never Last' away because it was too simple, but Waylon flipped over it." Jessi had originally written a song that went "Storms never last, do they Waylon?" and was going to toss it away when Waylon said, "Wait a minute, change that to 'baby.'"

"I don't even *try* to write songs with her any more," Waylon said, "because she just shoots right over my head. We wrote one song together and that's all. Her songs are real deep, and mine are more surface songs. Sometimes I'll read something she's written and ask her what it means, and when she explains it, I'll say, 'Well, I'll be' " (*Country Song Roundup*, January 1984).

Jessi enjoyed another country hit with "It's Morning (And I Still Love You)," which reached number eleven in early 1976, but since then she's had no more top-twenty records. Her songs have been recorded by Dottie West, Don Gibson, Anita Carter, Waylon, and many others.

Jessi Colter albums released since 1975's *I'm Jessi Colter* include *Jessi* and *Diamond in the Rough* (both 1976), *Mirriam* (1977), *That's the Way a Cowboy Rocks and Rolls* (1978), and *Ridin' Shotgun* (1982), all on Capitol Records. In 1980 she teamed with Waylon on the gold album *Leather and Lace* on RCA.

On Jessi's *Ridin' Shotgun* album her daughter Jennifer sings on the sweet song Jessi wrote for her, "Jennifer (Fly My Little Baby)." Waylon sings background on most of the album, including his own uptempo hit "Shine." Jennings produced the album with Randy Scruggs, son of the legendary bluegrass artist Earl Scruggs.

Though Waylon and Jessi had been singing together on stage over the previous twelve years, their first joint tour didn't come about until 1982, when they hit the road to promote *Leather and Lace* — and even then, they weren't singing many stage duets. Jessi opened the shows, followed by the Original Crickets. Waylon joined the Crickets at the end of their set and then did his own set, joined by Jessi for the finale.

How does Jessi like having a husband as her record

producer? "Waylon could have changed my whole style of writing and singing if he put his mind to it. But that is his beauty—he has that way of inspiring you without directing you. He is always super careful to avoid putting his stamp—of himself, that is—on somebody else. On me! That's why I insisted from the beginning that he work with me, produce me.

"Working with Waylon is exacting. He creates a lot of pressure. But I respect his artistic judgment."

Waylon said, "I try not to get too involved with Jessi's records, even though I help produce them. I try to stay out of it and let it go its own direction, to a point, and then I can help bring together what she and the musicians have got. If I go in and start arranging, it'll have my footprints all over it, and I don't want that" (*Family Weekly*, July 11, 1976).

You won't find a bigger Jessi Colter fan anywhere than Waylon Jennings. "She has an almost angelic voice. I think she's the greatest female singer there is because she's as original in her way as Mark Twain was in his.

". . . [C]ountry music is soul. And soul is Jessi Colter. She's got such a beautiful outlook on life that I think she was born half-high."

Jessi said she works hard to maintain a positive outlook on life. "Well, I just try to live a minute at a time. I refuse to be disappointed with anything. There is always a good side to every situation, and I look for that" (*Music City News*, June 1975).

"To tell you the truth, and I'm not always boastful, but creative men are harder to live with than others," Jessi stated. "It takes a lot of good sense and love. Yet it has a lot of rewards, and I wouldn't want it any other way."

Jessi staunchly defends her husband, who she says suffered at the hands of the Nashville System: "What you have to remember is that a lot of people have gone out of their way to hurt Waylon. When I first married him I was very naive to all of that. I just thought he was trying to do what he really believed in and was having a hard time of it.

"Then I realized there were all these people who didn't want him to do it. Who didn't want to see country music change at all" (*Miami News*, October 24, 1975).

Waylon is anything but an outlaw to Jessi's eyes. She sees him as a sensitive artist who knows music from both sides of the studio control board, as a considerate husband who loves to spend time at home, as a father who loves spending time with her and playing with Shooter, the only child from their sixteen-year marriage. (Between them Waylon and Jessi have six children and four grandchildren.)

Waylon says his children are "pretty cool" about having a country music star for a daddy. "They understand this whole bit . . . I say to people who work for me, 'You don't call them Waylon's Son or Waylon's Daughter. They have names, and you get who they are as individuals. Take them on their own terms.'

"They [the kids] think it's funny, the things that are written about me — the 'big, bad, mean' stuff, you know."

"They want to live their own lives," Jessi says. "They've got it together. When we come in off the road, we have to sit down and catch up on *them*" (*Family Weekly*, July 11, 1976).

Jessi said Waylon is an obsessive type, one who'll eat tuna fish every day for a year and after that never touch it again. "That's the way he is with his hobbies, his time-passers. It was pinball for a while, then . . . cards and dice."

"Age put some sense on him. There's been a settling in both of us. A lot of it has to do with the birth of Shooter. Having a child at that stage of our lives changed us both a lot" (*Palm Beach Post*, April 14, 1982).

Waylon and Jessi's son Shooter is a real joy in Waylon's life. Jennings is determined to be a better father this time around. "He's just a little fellow, but he's made a lot of changes," Waylon said.

At first Jessi was concerned about the effect of road life on Shooter growing up: "I talked to John Carter [Johnny Cash and June Carter Cash's son] to see what his memories were as a child traveling with his parents, because I was a little worried about having Shooter on the road.

"But John said he liked it. It was great fun, and he had a lot of support from the people in the crew. I feel being with your parents is the most important thing for a child, no matter where [the parents] are" (*Palm Beach Post*, April 14, 1982).

Since 1982, Jessi has devoted time and money to a Nashville YWCA job-readiness program aimed at women between the ages of eighteen and twenty-two. Jessi, who appeared in the *Tennessean* newspaper as recently as September 1985 to boost the Mothers and Daughters Are Worth It Campaign, said she became involved with the program after a talk with her then-eighteen-year-old daughter, Jennifer Harkness. "She expressed a desire that aside from her musical gifts, she really wanted to find something she enjoyed doing. Also, Waylon had another daughter at that age who had become a homemaker early without any training for a career."

Jessi said that after hearing of the YWCA program (which assists young women in communications skills, career exploration exercises, and on how to apply and interview for jobs), "My heart just kind of went out to the situation." She donated enough money to fund the program for a year.

"I'm so excited about this. I look at this and say I'm going to do this myself — and I've had a wonderful career and everything I need" (*Tennessean* July 4, 1982).

Waylon has always been quick to credit Jessi with bringing about a dramatic change in his life. ". . . I'd have to say, as far as changing my life goes, that knowing Jessi was the most important thing.

"I was on a collision course with something, I don't know what . . . when I met her. I really didn't care. Didn't figure anyone else did, either" (*Family Weekly*, July 11, 1976).

"She was like a buddy," Waylon said. "I'd be somewhere stoned and she'd set right there beside me like a little lady. And she'd let me know that I was all right. She'd talk to me and give me the confidence that I'd lost.

". . . It's hard to live up to what she thinks I can do. I've tried to tell her I ain't as much as she thinks I am. But I tell you, when somebody looks up at you and makes you feel very human and makes you feel good and feel that you are a good person, it can't do anything but help and be good for you.

"It's something I don't really understand. Like yesterday, I was a little bit down about something. And she comes up to me and says, 'Don't think a negative thought all the way through. Don't let it get complete. Now we're gonna think positive thoughts.' She's very smart. She don't know it, but she's smarter than I am in so many areas. But I ain't lettin' her know it" (*Houston Chronicle*, September 7, 1975).

Jessi says "it's my nature" to consider Waylon first. "It comes very naturally, very easily. As a result, he's

188

usually thinking for me, because he knows I'm always thinking of him first" (*Family Weekly*, July 11, 1976).

"It's his bus, his band, his decisions. I get to do all the fun things, like write and sing," she stated.

"I want [Jessi's] light to shine as bright as it will. I have a great time watching her develop. I'm not the male chauvinist pig people think I am. I believe in freedom," Waylon said.

". . . People used to ask me when Jessi had her first big pop hit, 'How does it feel when she has a pop hit right out of the shoot and you don't have one?'

" 'Well,' I says, 'being a god-damn legend, I don't really give a damn' " (*Minneapolis Star*, June 6, 1980).

"If it wasn't for her I wouldn't be here. Period. Physically, mentally, or any way."

Chapter Fifteen

"My Music's Got Me"

"I'll tell you, here's the best way to describe my situation. Some people have their music. My music's got me."
— Waylon Jennings
(*Cincinnati Enquirer*, December 10, 1983)

Since his first recording session with RCA in 1965, Waylon Jennings has recorded more than four hundred different songs, and has released about forty albums and sixty singles. His music touches on many styles, especially rock, blues, and country. His voice, though affected by years of hard living, remains a powerful instrument, still able to range from booming baritone to an eerie high register.

Waylon's voice is capable of expressing fear, irony, love, and humor in the same song—and of having you believe every word of it. His live shows are a mixture of sensitivity, tension, offhanded jokes tossed to the audience, and tight, powerful music delivered with a pulsating beat and compelling lyrics.

His music has progressed logically, from its roots, rather than through any sudden stylistic changes. Early cuts such as "Silver Ribbons" (1966) and "Mental Revenge" (1967) have glimmerings of the Waylon style that took form in the 1970s with "Ladies Love Outlaws" (1972) and continued in "I've Always Been Crazy" (1978).

Waylon rubbed Nashville's music establishment the wrong way for a number of years, and finally some of the labels that had been glued firmly on different musical styles began to wear off, and the old "star-maker" machinery began to creak. His musical "signature" did not develop overnight, and no one album or single is a pivotal point that shows where the man "socked it to the machine."

Though Waylon has released some inferior tracks and has not always stuck by this philosophy, here's his idea of what constitutes a good record: "The sound and feeling is as important as the words. A record should be like a mental picture. It should make a circle of live, style, and sound" (*Newsweek*, August 26, 1974).

The artificial restraints of country music's style and structure have always bothered Waylon as much as the corporate restrictions. ". . . I've always felt in country music we're locked into a three-chord progression and a kickoff with a fiddle and a steel turn-around, and that's a bunch of bull" (*Popular Music & Society*, No. 3, 1974). His 1961-65 experience in Phoenix shaped and flavored Waylon's musical style.

His music has won the acceptance of the music industry as well as record buyers—to date he has won two Grammy awards and four Country Music Association awards, in addition to logging about forty top-ten singles, seven gold (500,000 units sold) albums, and five albums that are each at least platinum (one million units sold).

Ironically, it was Waylon's songwriting that first drew him to the attention of RCA Records. Bobby Bare, who had recently recorded Waylon's "Just to Satisfy You," was impressed with Jennings's writing ability and voice, and told RCA's Chet Atkins about both.

Waylon has been writing songs since he was about twelve. His first song cut came at age twenty-one in 1958 when Frankie Miller recorded Jennings's composition "Young Widow Brown." Waylon later cut the song himself and included it on his *Love of the Common People* album.

"When I get to writing, it will come in spurts. Then, just like the others, the ones I consider the real writers, I figure that's the last song I'll ever write, because I just run the barrel dry. Then I go into a slump and don't write anything . . . That's why I like to hang out with writers — you inspire each other" (*Country Song Roundup*, January 1984).

In the mid-1960s in Phoenix, Waylon wrote about twenty songs with Don Bowman under the pseudonym of Jackson King, which he used while still under contract to A&M Records' Irving Music publishing company. Songs written with Bowman include "I Can't Get Over You," "Other You," "Kiss Me One More Time and Then," "Hurry Home to An Empty House," "Just Keep Reminding Me," "End Can't Be Far Away," "Best Friend You Ever Had," and better known ones such as "Just to Satisfy You" and "Anita, You're Dreaming." Waylon as Jackson King also wrote "We're Not Having Any Fun" with Harlan Howard. Tommy Cash recorded the Jackson King song "Wave Goodbye to Me" for a United Artists album.

By 1968 Waylon had written songs recorded by Bobby Bare, Johnny Cash, Glen Campbell, and others. One of the most successful early recordings of a Waylon Jennings-composed song (under the pseudonym of Jackson King) was Porter Wagoner's 1967 top-fifteen hit "Julie" (Waylon has a daughter named Julie, but says the song was not named for her). "My songs are all sort of personal statements," he says. "I just write down what I feel."

In the mid-1970s he admitted that his drug use had hampered his songwriting: "I'd love to write again the way I used to, and I think I'm getting there. I guess it's pretty well common knowledge that I went through a bad time, had some problems for a few years you know, pills and what-have-you.

"When you get into something like that it gets to the point where you don't think you can do anything without that crutch, and I really thought for a while I couldn't write any more . . ." (*Country Song Roundup* March 1975).

Waylon explained why he doesn't write songs with his wife Jessi: "I don't want to touch her style at all, and I'm pretty domineering myself when I'm in a studio. I mean, my footprints wind up in a studio if I'm there. And I don't want to do anything to make her [music] less pure" (*Aquarian*, February 24–March 3, 1982).

You never hear much about Waylon's abilities as a "picker," but he plays guitar, bass, mandolin, and a bit of fiddle, and his understanding of those instruments adds greatly to his skills as a producer. Unlike many other country stars, Waylon can provide his own instrumental punch with crisp guitar work. He repeatedly runs off riffs in his live shows and on record that let the listener know the guitar is not there just for decoration.

"He strums the instrument, almost passively, to sustain rhythm. Then, without noticeable animation, he somehow assaults the neck with incredible licks as fast as they are accurate. His punctuation is perfect. He swirls the ax into an amplifier, holding the pose to milk an exact feedback that sets a sound somewhere between psychedelic and autoharp" (*Tulsa Daily World*, February 14, 1976).

"As far back as I can remember, I was intrigued by guitar. I can remember when I was three, trying to get out of this jumper swing and reaching for my daddy's guitar—an old Gene Autry with a cowboy on a horse rearin' up" (*Guitar Player*, January 1984).

Jennings's electric guitar playing teeters in a delicate balance between punchy, 1950s-style rock guitar and a percussive style that has been dubbed chicken pickin'. That's Waylon you hear playing lead on many of his top hits, including "Luckenbach, Texas," "I've Always Been Crazy," "Theme From the Dukes of Hazzard," "Are You Sure Hank Done It This Way," and many others.

Guitar Player magazine noted "the way he has used the guitar to create reverberating walls of sound, from the acoustic blues-based *This Time* to the modern rock-toned *Black on Black* to the crackling country twang of *It's Only Rock and Roll*."

His guitar playing is influenced by Buddy Holly, to the extent that it relies heavily on electric rhythms. But Waylon has added his own string bending, blues phrasing, and pedal steel techniques (after years of playing on stage with the master Ralph Mooney) to create his own lean, muscular style of playing.

Jennings says his playing is also influenced by black music: "Back in Texas I used to listen to KWKH in Shreveport, Louisiana, to 'Stan the Man and His No-Name Record Jive.' That was before rock 'n roll, and he'd play Bobby 'Blue' Bland and B.B. King.

"[In Littlefield] I used to deliver ice in what they called Black Town, and I'd go to a place called the Dew Drop Inn. I met this guy who called himself Chuck Berry Jr., and he taught me to use a banjo string for the high E on the guitar and move the rest of the strings up. That way I could bend the strings . . . that's really when I started playing lead guitar" (*Guitar Player*, January 1984).

A big fan of songwriters, Waylon has recorded many tunes by Billy Joe Shaver, Shel Silverstein, Harlan Howard, and others, as well as tunes by unknowns whose work he admires. "I'll tell you what I am. I'm an interpreter. I like to take another's man's song and make it sound like I wrote it. I'm a fan of writers" (Bane).

Waylon admits to being a perfectionist when it comes to putting his music on tape: "Somebody just has to get hold of me and pull me out of [the studio], 'cause I could just go on and on foolin' with sounds. I always seem to think it's not quite good enough . . . that I could work longer and harder and make it better. But maybe not" (*Pittsburgh Press*, January 16, 1983).

"I'm very hard to please. I'm particular. I pick at everything around me. It has to be good, right, and original, and soulful before I dig it" (*Door*, December 9–23, 1971).

He keeps an edge on his music "by trying to surprise myself. I very seldom learn a song until I get in the studio, and then I work off the inspiration. On stage, I never plan a show. I let it happen as I feel it. It keeps the band awake" (*Cincinnati Enquirer*, December 10, 1983). He likes the "freshness and the little insecurities" that result from playing and recording material he doesn't completely know. Even his own compositions — he often tucks songs away after writing them so he forgets them. He has on occasion cut a song after writing it on the way to the studio.

"If I like a song, I learn it quickly. Then we run it down two or three times and cut it. After that, I start messing with it, trying to do different things. . . . After I'm done, though, I don't listen to a record that much. For some reason, it seems like it don't belong to me anymore.

"The studio's a controlled atmosphere. It's hard to work in, but it's my favorite part of what I do, recording. I like everybody on the project to be involved, too. 'What do you think?' I ask everybody, and I ride 'em till they ride me.

"They come to realize that I'm serious. I really want to know — I want their ideas. I'm totally [involved] in the music. When I'm in Nashville, I go session-hopping sometimes. I'm on a lot of records people don't know I'm on, but that's what it's all about" (*Dallas Times Herald*, November 13, 1983).

Waylon loves to experiment with drum rhythms in the recording studio, and he can never get enough guitar sounds on his records, sometimes overdubbing six or seven guitars to achieve the desired effect.

Waylon Jennings stage shows have in the past alternated between crisp brilliance and dull indifference. Much of this was probably due to his heavy tour schedules — and his heavy drug use. He never has believed in talking much between songs on stage. ". . . [I]'ve seen so many country acts in particular that will sing themselves right on top and then talk theirselves [sic] right into a hole and just bury it. So it's still like in radio when, I remember, I used to work with this hard-nosed dude, man, but he taught me a lot [about] radio. Like . . . if ya ain't got something that's funny, informative, or important, then shut up" (*Popular Music & Society*, No. 3, 1974).

He says he wants individualists in his band, people who are their own men, with their own thoughts. "I don't want to do anything that takes away from that. Because I had to take orders for too long myself not to know what's it's like" (Guralnick).

Waylon likes to take another writer's song and give it such a personal interpretation it sounds like he wrote it. He calls it "making it his own" song. "I did one of Jessi's songs and she said, 'It's good, but it's not yours yet.' That's why I love to do other people's material—to try to sing it to a point where it sounds as if I wrote it, not to take anything away from them" (*Minneapolis Star*, June 6, 1980).

Though at the peak of the outlaw phase he crossed over onto the pop charts, Waylon will never be a pop artist—and he doesn't want to be. "With Willie, what you see is what you get. He's just what he appears to be. I ain't got time for all that, anyway. I'm not lookin' for crossover hits. I'm not gonna cross over to them. They gotta come here" (*Dallas Times Herald*, November 13, 1983).

He has always had strong opinions about what makes a song "country": "If you think a beat or an instrument or a chord progression or a kazoo makes country music or pop, you don't know what country is—it's the soul of the singer" (*Newsweek*, August 26, 1974).

"Country music is soul music. It can't be done with lyrics, with chord progression or with psychedelics. (Associated Press interview, mid-1973).

". . . [T]he term country music covers a lot of territory, all the way from bluegrass to what they call contemporary or uptown. There's an awful lot in between. The thing that I'm doing is just 'my thing,' and if you want to label it, it's 'my kind of country.'

"There are some people who say I use too heavy a beat and too many instruments . . . but if instruments and beats made our music then we'd be in trouble anyway.

"Country music is like black man's blues. They are only a beat apart. It's the same man, singing the same song, about his same problems, and his loves, his losses, the good and the bad times" (*Country Song Roundup*, March 1975).

Waylon Jennings will no doubt be in the Country Music Hall of Fame some day, where his plaque will be placed alongside those of his childhood idols Jimmie Rodgers, Hank Williams, Bob Wills, and others. But sales and awards aren't uppermost on Waylon's mind. "You've got to *care*. You've got to care about the music. You work with other musicians who care, and your audience cares. You better care too, hoss, and if you don't, you shouldn't be doing it.

"You'd better not be doing it for the publicity, the fame or the money. And you'd *sure* better not be doing it because it's a way to make a living, 'cause that ain't always going to be easy. You got to believe it, believe in the music" (*Country Song Roundup*, January 1984).

"I hate to say anything Mac Davis ever said, but I believe in music. It's one of the real hopes of the world. I've been where we've got people together under one roof of different races, creeds and walks of life without any problems. Religion and politics haven't been able to do that" (*Minneapolis Star*, June 6, 1980).

"I do know that, in spite of everything, I've had a

good time, and that I'm still as big a fan of music, of songwriters, as ever. When I hear a great song for the first time, I still get as excited as I ever did. And when something comes off good in the studio, I know it excites me as much as ever.

"As far as recording and touring go, if I'm home more than a week at a time, I start walking the floor. I have no intentions of retiring, no way!"

Chapter Sixteen

Who Is the Real Waylon Jennings?

Who is the real Waylon Jennings? In many ways what you see is what you get — Waylon is what you hear in his music, and what you read about him in the papers. Music is his work, recreation, and motivation. But there are other aspects to Waylon's personality that only emerge when you find out about the kind-hearted, behind-the-scenes help he has given to others.

When you begin to get behind the public image and learn who the real Waylon Jennings is, you learn that he is a shy and humble man who has never forgotten where he came from, and who feels genuine concern for anyone born with one or two strikes against him or her because of physical or economic handicaps.

A close associate said of Jennings, "I've seen Waylon read something in the newspaper that affects him deeply, and he'll get right up and do something about it. He won't let anyone know about it, not even the person he helped. He's like an undercover angel. The world would be shocked if it knew all the good things he has done for people."

"Here's a side a Waylon you don't ever see written

about," said Larry Corbin, who knew Waylon from the KLLL days in Lubbock. "In 1970 a tornado hit Lubbock and destroyed much of the downtown area. We built a new memorial civic center, and Waylon was the first act to play it. He wouldn't take any money for doing the show, not even to cover expenses.

"After the concert we drove out to the Boy's Ranch east of Lubbock, and Waylon presented them with a check for $20,000. He didn't want anyone to know about it."

He's a man who has done a whole lot of living. You can see that in the deep creases around Waylon's eyes. He'll sit with his elbows on the table and lean forward as he talks to you, putting you on the spot if he doesn't agree with you, but without meanness. He peppers his talk on and off stage with quirky, off-handed remarks, most of them humorous.

Waylon's a man of odd contradictions, one who shuns interviews — but then is surprisingly candid when he does talk to the press. At its best his music mirrors Waylon's inner feelings, a complex mixture of bewilderment, rage, strength, weakness. Like Waylon, his music can be open-minded or opinionated, harsh or kind-spoken.

Peter Guralnick said of Jennings in *Lost Highway*: "He's above all uncompromisingly honest and open in a way that allows him to say 'Hey, I love you' to a buddy without having you suspect either his honesty or his protective machismo."

Most people only see the image Waylon projects on stage, and that image is somewhat sinister, with his long hair flowing out from under a dark hat, a scraggly beard, solemn eyes, leather vest, and worn jeans, usually with a cigarette clenched between his teeth. "I don't worry about images. I'm the same person whether I'm singing on-stage or whether I'm off-stage. I really could never live being two or three different-type people" (*Penthouse*, September 1981).

Few realize that offstage Waylon Jennings is actually a shy person, one who's had to find a way to endure the acclaim that comes with being a music star. One writer, referring to Waylon's *Lonesome, On'ry and Mean* album title, said after meeting Waylon, "It's easy to see why 'Personable, Reasonable, Friendly, and Polite' wouldn't be a scorcher on the record charts, but that's really a much better description of Jennings."

"It's a funny thing," Waylon said, "but people in general make me nervous. Now this is a hell of a business to be in with that kind of attitude, isn't it?" (*Miami News*, October 24, 1975).

"If it [success] was a bit less, I think I'd be more comfortable with it. I'm an introverted person in an extroverted business. It gets hard to handle every once in a while. . . . Sometimes I feel trapped by success."

Waylon said that at the height of his "outlaw" fame, ". . . I started realizing I didn't want a lot of things that came with being a star. I liked it when I could run loose, when I could just go out and play pinball and whatever. But things are getting better. I have good people working with me. They take away a lot of the strain" (*Minneapolis Star*, July 24, 1978).

"If nobody recognized me or said anything to me I'm sure it would bother me . . . [b]ut now, it bothers me so much more to be this way. You know, I'm bashful. I'm shy, I really am. . . . I have to almost *feel* a person to trust them, before I can open up and talk to them. And I don't know what to say when somebody says they like my records. Except 'thank you.' If I ain't got no rocks to kick and say, 'Aw, shit,' I'm in trouble" (Bane).

Waylon is the greatest critic of his own work. In the February 16, 1974, *Record & Radio Mirror*, Waylon said that in the previous eight years, ". . . I've cut one or two things I've been pretty happy with, but as far as I can remember, nothing that has made me completely happy all the way through. The closest I came was with 'Good Hearted Woman.'

"But I don't guess I'll ever be satisfied. If I am I'll probably go into another business, because if you're ever satisfied, it means you're not very interested any more. There ain't nobody who ever gets it right."

Two of Waylon's enduring "hobbies" are sports and studying and analyzing the lives of famous people. He says he started the latter when he was about twenty-four, "when I realized that everybody is an individual." Both hobbies come together in Waylon's appreciation of Muhammad Ali.

While Kris Kristofferson was in New Orleans a few years ago making a movie with Muhammad Ali, Waylon asked him to get a pair of Ali's boxing gloves, which are now in Waylon's museum in Nashville. To Waylon, Ali is "the man of the decade." Why? Waylon identifies with Ali's struggle with The System. "He let them take away his title, something he had worked his whole life for, rather than give up his belief," Waylon explained. "Muhammad could have taken the easy way out. He could have just done a few exhibition bouts overseas, but he didn't. He stood his ground. You've got to admire someone who'll do that" (*Minneapolis Star*, July 24, 1978).

"We [Ali and Waylon] were sitting on a bench a few minutes before the [Ali vs. Spinks] fight, and the television people kept trying to shove me out of the way so they could film Ali. After a little bit, Ali said in that joking way of his, 'Waylon! Don't let 'em talk to you like that! Slap 'em! Slap 'em, Waylon!' " (*Country Music*, January/February 1979).

Ali came to Nashville for Shooter's christening in mid-1979. While he was in town he took a turn driving Waylon's bus.

There's no doubt who Waylon's biggest hero is, though: "[T]he greatest man I ever knew was my dad, and he was a really religious man, he just didn't do wrong. And he didn't think I did too much wrong, either.

"A while before he died, we got to be really good friends, we really understood each other, and he'd always try to figure out some way to help me justify any mistake I'd made. That's the kind of man he was" (*Photoplay*, February 1975).

Waylon has always been the first to admit he's not the most ambitious person. "No, I don't guess I am, maybe that's one of my problems. I'm the only thing I could have been, so how can you be ambitious when you're that way? I think the art is more important to me than the stardom. That may sound corny to some people" (*Country Music People*, July 1971).

"Success? I can't even tell you where my records are on the charts. Somebody at the record company will take care of that for me. I'm not trying to be Number One. I'm not trying to be the greatest. Once you're there, then what?" (*Dallas Times Herald*, November 13, 1983).

Waylon often helps people out with money, a gift, or a phone call, always insisting that either the person he helps doesn't know who did the giving, or that there be no publicity about the event.

Waylon comforted a Tulsa truck driver who was seriously injured in an accident in the spring of 1979 by phoning the trucker from Dallas. The man's wife had managed to get word to Waylon that he was the trucker's idol, and that a phone call would help his spirits.

In the April 6, 1979, Oklahoma City *Oklahoman* the trucker's wife said Waylon asked if her husband Larry could talk. The hospital representative on the other end of the line told Waylon no. So a nurse held the phone up to Larry's ear and Jennings talked to him for about ten minutes.

Waylon toured the Shawnee County (Kansas) jail in June 1979 and chatted with inmates and local law enforcement officers. He was promoting an all-inmate rodeo being held to raise funds to establish a Kansas Sheriffs' Youth Ranch.

"I was in a few scrapes as a kid," Waylon said, "and I know that if you just take one step in the wrong direction, it's hard to get back on the right track. I know that I had a lot of help myself, and I appreciated it . . ." (Topeka *Daily Capital*, June 10, 1979).

Waylon Jennings, George Jones, Johnny Cash, Tammy Wynette, and others performed on the Grand Ole Opry stage in a February 1980 concert held to raise money for the Hundred Club, which helps Nashville families of firefighters and policemen killed in the line of duty.

In May 1980 Waylon comforted a dying man by visiting him at his home in Raleigh, North Carolina. Cancer victim Joel Jackson lay at home in bed while his idol, Waylon, and his entourage rolled up outside in two buses. A friend of the family had arranged the visit a week earlier when she flew to Charlotte, North

Carolina, and met with Jennings at his concert there.

Jackson's dream came true when the bearded Jennings walked into the house. Wearing his familiar vest, boots, and black hat, and accompanied by Waylors Albright, Mooney, and Gordon Payne, Jennings walked up to Jackson, stuck out his hand, and said "Joel, I'm Waylon Jennings, and I'm proud to meet you."

Waylon chatted with the man for about forty-five minutes. A member of the entourage said, "Jackson offered Waylon a beer and he accepted it, even though he doesn't drink. He held it all the while he talked with the man." Just hours later Jackson died of the cancer he had battled for seven years.

In March 1984 Waylon donated $1,000 to help a young namesake in West Virginia, a five-year-old boy who suffered from a usually fatal form of bone cancer.

The check was sent to Waylon Rose's elementary school in Alum Bridge, with the stipulation that it be spent for toys and clothes. The boy's father and mother were great fans of Jennings, and had named their son for him.

Don't think Waylon is mellowing in all ways—he's still outspoken on many issues.

He broke a seven-year boycott to appear on the Country Music Association's televised award show in October 1984, but he has never been a rousing supporter of the organization, or of any other organization that devotes so much attention to bestowing awards. "I don't like the whole thing about it. I don't agree with the way the CMA [Country Music Association] decides on Artist of the Year . . . It's block voting, where corporations, the record companies

. . . have so many employees, they all get to sign their ballot and have a vote. They get to sign their ballot and send it back [to the company]. The number one vote is put in afterward" (*Tennessean*, July 9, 1983).

Waylon's observation about block voting was true. This and other complaints led to change in CMA voting rules that limit the impact that a single company can have on the awards. The CMA has since made other changes in its voting rules to avoid problems with block voting.

Through the years Waylon has also been bothered by the fact that the CMA does little to help new artists (though it now exposes more up-and-coming major-label artists on its TV show): "What matters is when a new artist is involved. Those [awards] could be such an encouragement to them. If they [CMA] have an awards program, they ought to give it to the younger ones, the ones who are starting out. I remember when it would have meant something to me. But it doesn't any more" (*Minneapolis Star*, July 24, 1978).

Waylon and others also wonder, "How come Hank Williams Jr., who has more albums on the charts than anybody (he had seven on the charts at one point in 1982), how come he hasn't won a CMA award? Something is wrong, because Hank is a *great* artist . . ." (*Country Song Roundup*, January 1984).

Waylon is not impressed with the quality of programming on the Nashville Network cable operation, which was launched by the same company that owned the Grand Ole Opry from its inception. "[Nashville Network is] like a country imitation of big-time Hollywood. It's not good enough. You have to live with everything you do. That's like putting out bad records. I just think we've got a lot more to offer than something like that" (*Tennessean*, July 9, 1983).

"A lot of times they do country music things on low budgets, and it really shows. They should take a few more minutes, some more time. It only costs 100 percent to go first class" (*Tennessean*, June 16, 1984).

Two of Waylon's biggest pet peeves are organized religion and TV evangelists. "I think organized religion is in trouble. I think you're in trouble if you believe in organized religion. If you have the church door open and don't make black people feel welcome in a white man's church, that's wrong. I don't want to go to their heaven . . .

"I think [TV evangelists are] sick, man. Like Jim Bakker—he sits there and begs and cries for money. He's asking for money from these people that are sending in their Social Security checks to him while his wife is sitting there with diamonds on big enough to choke a horse and sings a half-tone sharp, when she gets that close to it" (*Tennessean*, July 9, 1983).

"I always felt this way: if they didn't like the way I was as a person, then they could keep the hell away from me. I'll pay the piper myself. . . . [T]he way I am, the way I live, is just not any of their damn business" (*Penthouse*, September 1981).

"I ain't never been like very many people anyway, you know. Actually, I'm in my own mold. Maybe y'all are the rebels and I'm not" (*Miami Herald*, December 9, 1979).

A good account of the impact Waylon had on country music from 1965–75 is revealed in a comment that Hank Williams Jr. makes in his autobiography, *Living Proof*: "So Waylon beat 'em, I can't tell you what that meant to me. Because if Waylon could beat 'em, I could beat 'em."

Romantic misfit . . . rebel . . . outlaw . . . or maverick, Waylon remains a reminder that you don't always have to adapt to The Way Things Are Right Now.

"If there was ever any message I was trying to get across to people, it's a simple one. The message is just that no matter what you're trying to do in life, there is another way—*your* way. And everyone, whether it's you or me or anybody, has a right to try it at least once in their life."

Chapter Seventeen

"Pushin' 50 and Still Wearin' Jeans"

"I never wanted to destroy anything. It's called survival. I don't think people really understood what I was trying to do. A lot of folks were afraid I was trying to destroy something, but actually, I was just trying to do things the best way I could. . . . I just couldn't go along with the way things were being done."
— Waylon Jennings
(*Aquarian* February 24–March 3, 1982)

Waylon Arnold Jennings at age forty-eight is actually a shy man, still somewhat uncomfortable with the star role, a man who'd much rather talk about his music than himself.

He has logged a few million miles on the concert trail, playing skull orchards and major civic arenas, staying in countless hotels. He has added a few pounds along the way, and lost a bit of the vocal power that marked his releases in the 1960s and 1970s.

Waylon stands alongside such veterans as George Jones, Willie Nelson, and Merle Haggard as a symbol of rugged authenticity in an increasingly complex country music scene where the music often strays from its simple roots and some artists get their personalities from Plastics, Unltd.

Waylon's other 1984 album, *Greatest Hits, Vol. II*, contained two new tracks that went top-ten as singles. "America," written by Sammy Johns, peaked at number six in December 1984. Jennings's spring 1985 single, "Waltz Me to Heaven," penned by Dolly Parton, was a warm tune about a happy man who's taking his lover for a spin around the dance floor — not your typical Waylon song! It's done in straight ³/₄ time, also unusual for Jennings recording, as he often prefers to add cross-rhythms. "Waltz Me" reached number ten in April 1985.

In the spring of 1985, the Showtime cable network aired "Cowboy in London," a 60-minute Waylon Jennings concert taped at the Hammersmith Odeon theater.

As this is being written Waylon is putting the finishing touches on his *Turn the Page* album. The LP was recorded in 1984 during a period when Waylon was devoting all his energy and attention to kicking drugs, so it contains no new Jennings compositions.

An interesting note: In the first quarter of 1985, with country record sales suffering from their second major slump in three years, there were only three albums that received RIAA (Recording Industry Association of America) platinum certification — all three were Waylon Jennings albums: *Wanted! The Outlaws*, *Greatest Hits* and *Waylon & Willie*. (Each album was already platinum-certified and passing a new platinum milestone).

*　*　*

Waylon Jennings has been called many things, but he's never been called bland. If Waylon was a rebel, he was rebelling against the packaging, homogenization, and inconsiderate treatment that recording artists were getting in Nashville.

His independence and different outlook on music made him a maverick from the beginning, in the eyes of the Nashville music establishment. He didn't wear the rhinestone suits that were a "must" for country stars of the 1960s. He didn't tell corny jokes between songs on stage. When others were singing "Rocky Top" he was singing "Norwegian Wood" and "Mac-Arthur Park."

The music that resulted from Waylon's struggle for artistic freedom found a lot of fans, in and out of the music industry—to date he has won four CMA awards (including 1975's honor as Best Male Vocalist), and Grammys in 1969 and 1978. "Compromising is awful hard when you have no reverse. The system is at fault because they [the Nashville establishment] are afraid of destroying it. Consequently, you destroy yourself because the system won't be destroyed. It still works. What really matters is controlling your own destiny and your own life" (*Minneapolis Star*, June 6, 1980).

Waylon has charted more than fifty-five singles, more than thirty of which reached top five, with more than a dozen hitting number one in music trade magazines, including his duets with Willie Nelson such as "Mammas Don't let Your Babies Grow Up to Be Cowboys" and "Good Hearted Woman." His most recent solo number one is 1982's "Lucille."

According to RCA Records, Jennings has total career sales in excess of sixteen million units. He has three multi-platinum albums: *Waylon's Greatest Hits* (quadruple platinum, or four million units sold), *Wanted! The Outlaws* and *Waylon & Willie* (each double platinum), as well as platinum albums *Ol' Waylon* and *I've Always Been Crazy.*

Seven of Waylon's albums have gone gold, registering sales in excess of 500,000 units. His 1980 smash "The Theme from the Dukes of Hazzard (Good Ol' Boys)" is his first and only platinum (two million units sold) single.

In spite of his rebellious image Waylon's not really a rebel. He has remained friends even with those he disagreed with through the years—Chet Atkins, Chips Moman, Alan Cartee—he and Tompall speak now and then. In late 1984 Waylon resolved a long-standing dispute with his former manager Neil Reshen, though he will probably never work with Reshen again. Waylon is friends with Duane Eddy, Jessi's former husband. And listen to this, folks—the outlaw is in his sixteenth year of marriage to Jessi.

On top of that, Waylon recently celebrated his twentieth anniversary with RCA Records, his one and only Nashville label. But, by late 1985 he was preparing to change labels.

Waylon and Willie had a couple of minor spats through the years, most notably over Willie's annual picnic—which Waylon thought was getting too big, messy, and commercialized—and about Neil Reshen. According to Larry Corbin, Waylon's friend from the KLLL-Lubbock days, when Willie distanced himself from Neil and suggested that Waylon do the same, Waylon got irked because "he thought Willie wasn't being loyal to Neil." Waylon later changed his mind and dropped Reshen as well.

The rock influence in Waylon's music offended some country purists initially—but through the years it's become apparent that Waylon *is* country, and not a "crossover" artist.

Waylon paved the way for other artists by winning the right to choose his own material and studio musicians, to produce his own records, to chart his own musical course. "I never set out to change anything. But you know, every business has its system that works for eighty percent of the people who are in it. But there's always that other twenty percent who just don't fit in. That's what happened to me, and it happened to Johnny Cash, and it happened to Willie Nelson. We just couldn't do it the way it was set up. I was just doin' things the way I had to. . . . But when you walk your own path, there's often resentment. There's often a big price to pay."

Waylon still shuns as many of the trappings of stardom as he can. He hardly ever does an interview. He has learned to pace himself, and it took him years to get used to the idea that he's in the driver's seat. "I have come to the conclusion the business can run you to death if you try to keep up with it. Let it keep up with you. If you worry about energies and worry about how big you are going to be, where is that at?" (*Country Music*, January/February 1979).

Jennings does fewer concerts now, but for good money. Instead of the three hundred dates a year he did in the late 1960s, he's now doing about a hundred and twenty dates a year, including better-paying fairs, getting from $15,000 to $25,000 per night, depending on the show and circumstances. Waylon's show has changed little, though now that the Original Crickets have disbanded it consists of Waylon, Jessi, and the Waylors.

Waylon still spends a lot of time on his bus — playing a dice game he helped invent called "farkle," watching yet another rerun of a western such as *Law of the Lash.*

In Nashville, Jennings enjoys relaxing in the privacy of his inner sanctum, a plush second-story office at his business headquarters at 1117 17th Avenue South on Music Row. His publishing company, production company, and other businesses have been run since 1977 from this comfortable old brick building, previously a small Victorian-style mansion. It still has a number of elegant wood-mantled fireplaces and crystal chandeliers, tastefully intermingled with security cameras and closed-circuit TV monitors. Marylou Hyatt, who has worked for Waylon since 1977, was recently promoted from being his business manager to president and chief executive officer of WGJ ("Waylon Goddamn Jennings") Productions.

Behind the large antique wooden desk in Waylon's office is a sign that says "This Is No Dress Rehearsal. We Are Professionals. This Is The Big Time." Waylon laughs and says the sign is for *him*, not his staff. His suite features blue suede curtains and walls, a bumper pool room, a video viewing room with a giant screen, and other film and video equipment.

Waylon, Jessi, Shooter, and assorted children live in the Brentwood suburb about fifteen miles from Nashville. Jennings occasionally commutes to his Music Row office in the vintage 1959 Cadillac Coupe deVille that Hank Williams Jr. gave him.

Since October of 1983 Waylon's concert engagements have been co-booked exclusively by Buddy Lee Attractions of Nashville and Mark Rothbaum and Associates of Danbury, Connecticut. Rothbaum, previously an aide to Waylon's 1970s manager Neil Reshen, books and manages Willie Nelson, as well as country outlaw David Allan Coe.

Advising Waylon on other important career matters are his attorney/co-manager Gerry Margolis, and TV agent/co-manager Bill Robinson, both of Los Angeles. Jessi Colter still writes songs and records regularly, though she does not have a label deal at this time.

Waylon is a grandfather four times over from children by his previous marriages.

Terry Jennings, twenty-eight, is married, lives in Fort Worth and has two children. Julie, twenty-seven, lives in Nashville and has one child. Buddy, twenty-four, recently graduated from South Plains Junior College in Levelland, Texas, twenty miles south of Littlefield. Shooter Jennings, six, plays drums, and in early 1985 was delighted to be given a guitar just like his daddy's.

Jennifer, twenty-one, Jessi's child by Duane Eddy, is attending Belmont College in Nashville. Divorced, she has one child. Tomi, also twenty-one, adopted by Waylon and Lynne, is living and working in Arizona.

Years before he reached his present state of equilibrium, Waylon had the right idea about bringing up his kids: "I have a good relationship with my children. They've had a rough time, and I'm sorry about that. It took me so long to get together anything resembling a family life that they've had it bad. There's been a lot of hurt on their mother's side and on mine, too, and then they've had to live with a lot because of who I am and what I do. . . .

"I want them to figure out what *they* want. If I can help them, I will, but I just want them to be happy, really, really I do, and be good" (*Photoplay*, February 1975).

"When I was growing up, we didn't give a damn about the government. We didn't pay no attention to it, and we weren't really worried about it. But in the past twenty years the kids have become very aware

216

and concerned about the rights and the wrongs. And for that reason I think we're in pretty good shape" (*Penthouse*, September 1981).

Waylon's father died in 1968. His mother, Lorene, now about sixty-five, remarried and lives in Littlefield with her second husband, James Gilbert. Also in Littlefield are Waylon's youngest brother Bo, who works on oil rigs, and next to the youngest James D., who owns a service station and a fair amount of real estate in the area.

Tommy Jennings, a year younger than Waylon, lives near Nashville, and continues to work in the music industry. Tommy charted in the nineties in 1975 with "Make It Easy on Yourself" on Paragon Records, and in the seventies with "Don't You Think It's Time" on Monument in 1978. He went into the fifties in 1980 with Rex Gosdin with "Just Give Me What You Think Is Fair," on Sabre.

Tommy's latest entry on the charts was as co-producer, publisher, and writer of Johnny Paycheck's early 1985 single, "I Never Got Over You." Tommy has also been at work on an album of his own, which he plans to call "The Angel and the Dollar Bill."

"This is the first chance I've had to build a record the way I want," said Tommy, echoing the words of his brother from more than a decade earlier. "We don't have to go by a record company's rules until we get it completed. You got to realize that when you talk to the head of a record label today, a lot of times you're talking to an accountant."

A pleasant man with a quiet, sincere manner, Tommy has never tried to link his career to Waylon's. "If I was working shows with [Waylon], I probably would feel overshadowed. That's why I'm not working shows with him. He's big, and I'm proud of him. But where I've gone I've done it on my own with the help of some good friends.

"We're like brothers at the house. But in the business we're like two guys in a shop doing the best they can" (*Roanoke Times & World News*, January 21, 1979).

None of the clubs that Waylon played most often during his years in Phoenix has survived the times. J.D.'s, the largest of the lot, later became the Whiskey River club, which was gutted by fire in the early 1980s. Waylon's former DJ-and-songwriting pal Don Bowman became a standup comic and opened shows for Eddy Arnold, Merle Haggard, and Willie Nelson. He now lives in Austin, Texas.

Chet Atkins produces an occasional record and continues to perform and record, having switched from RCA to CBS Records. He is a member of the Country Music Hall of Fame. Neil Reshen is still in Danbury, Connecticut, and says he runs an artist management firm called Dawn Management, though he declined to name his clients, and no such company is listed in the Manhattan phone directory.

Larry Corbin runs a stock brokerage in Ruidoso, New Mexico. His brother Sky runs a small radio station in Oklahoma. Ray "Slim" Corbin was shot and killed in 1971 in Phoenix by a woman who became infatuated with him while he was performing at Mr. Magoo's club there.

Diagnosed as a borderline diabetic in 1981, Waylon takes no medicine for the condition — he controls it with his diet. "He leads a more relaxed, controlled life now," a close associate said. He plays only ninety to a hundred and twenty dates a year. He gets more sleep, and watches his diet, though he has gained weight, one of the results of kicking drugs. Jennings enjoys his family, and when he's not on the road he enjoys a lifestyle that's about as casual as you can get. Waylon could alter a line from his number-one single "Amanda" and it would be an apt description of him: "I'm pushin' 50 and still wearin' jeans."

Waylon has been drug-free since March 31, 1984. He says he is being open about his addiction because he hopes his story might help others. "I could sit and talk till I was blue in the face to people who are still hooked, and all they'd do is resent it. But if, by speaking out, I can convince just one person not to try drugs or get on them in the first place, then I'll feel like I've done some good."

As always, he credits Jessi for standing by him: "She never gave up on me, and it was her positive attitude toward life that finally pulled me through. She went through things that no woman should have to go through to live with a man. But she stuck by me. She saved my life.

"My life's got a whole new direction to it now. It feels great to be a part of the human race again! Everything I do now, that I used to think I couldn't do without drugs—performing, recording—now I can do *better*. Everything is just so much easier, and I enjoy it so much now! It's like waking up in a whole new world every morning now."

On first thought Waylon Jennings seems to be one of the least likely stars to create his own tourist attraction. But that's just what Waylon did in June 1984, when the "Waylon's Private Collection" museum opened its doors on Music Row.

It's an unusual move for one of music's most publicity-shy stars, a singer who for the past twenty-five years had resisted every effort to run a fan club on his behalf. But Waylon said he had been kicking the idea around for years, just waiting for the right location (it's upstairs from the Country Music Wax Museum).

Among Waylon's favorite items on display in the museum are Buddy Holly's motorcycle, Willie Nelson's braids, the pair of Hank Williams boots given to him by Hank Jr., Muhammad Ali's boxing gloves, Waylon's car collection (including the General Lee car from "Dukes of Hazzard"), and a clip of his movie debut in 1966's *Nashville Rebel*. Also on display are letters and other objects from Jessi Colter, John Lennon, Hank Williams, George Jones, Hank Williams Jr., and other celebrities.

Waylon traveled to Switzerland in December 1984 to appear with Willie Nelson, Kris Kristofferson, and others in a Johnny Cash Christmas special shot there. Waylon also gave Cash a cameo appearance in Jennings's "Album Flash" video promoting the *Never Could Toe the Mark* album on Cinemax cable TV.

As he gained confidence in his new career effort and recovery from drugs, Waylon appeared on the Grand Ole Opry, sang "America" on the CMA's televised awards show in October 1984, and in early 1985 performed "America" on the "12th Annual American Music Awards" TV show in Los Angeles.

While Jennings and Cash were in New York in early February 1985 for three nights of concerts at Radio City Music Hall, they appeared on national TV on the "David Letterman Show" and "Saturday Night Live." On the former Waylon joined Cash in singing a Kris Kristofferson song, then talked about kicking drugs. In the latter Billy Crystal walked up to him in the audience and subjected Waylon to some good-natured ribbing about his hat and appearance.

Waylon, Cash, Willie, and Kris Kristofferson joined forces to record a quartet album and video called *The Highwayman*, which CBS released in

April 1985. Waylon sings on the title track, as well as "Last Cowboy Song," "Big River," "Welfare Line," "Against the Wind," and the "Desperados Waiting for a Train." The album went number one.

Today Waylon is having more fun than ever on stage. The February 13, 1985, *Variety* said of his concert with Cash at Radio City Music Hall that "it's obvious to one who has seen them perform together any number of times—particularly Jennings—that there has been a marvelous transformation, even a metamorphosis . . .

"What was onstage . . . was a party attitude and a loose performance which was as much fun to watch and listen to as it obviously was to join in . . . Jennings sounded great throughout, working easily with an excellent backup unit, and easing through a lot of newer material before reprising some of the hits he scored alone and with the likes of Willie Nelson."

At a recent Midwest concert, Waylon called Jessi out on stage and kidded her good-naturedly about her good looks. In the middle of singing "Good Hearted Woman" he asked the audience if they wanted to hear Willie's part—and then did an excellent imitation of Nelson by using a finger to hold one nostril shut as he sang.

Jennings is also playing dates with Willie Nelson again, opening the show, as he does for Cash. The Jennings/Nelson concert has been described as a Waylon Jennings concert, followed by a Willie Nelson show. Their duets are far from being the evening's highlight, still representing more a musical statement than works of beauty.

Willie continues to be one of the hottest artists in any field of music, always experimenting, always at or near the top of the charts. He had an across-the-boards country/pop/easy listening hit with Julio Iglesias in mid-1984 ("To All the Girls I've Loved Before"), and later that year had seven albums at the same time on *Billboard*'s country album chart, including duet LPs with Kris and Merle.

Waylon has recently devoted much attention to supporting the Sue Brewer Fund, in memory of a friend of Nashville songwriters of the 1960s and 1970s who died of cancer in June 1981. Waylon, Kris Kristofferson, Willie Nelson, Hank Cochran, Shel Silverstein, and other stars donated their time and talents to a two-hour TV special "The Door Is Always Open," taped in the fall of 1984 for airing as a syndicated show in 1985. Each artist on the show was helped in some way by Sue Brewer, who never locked the door to her apartment near Nashville's Music Row, and who often gave struggling songwriters something to eat, a place to sleep, and encouragement in their work.

"When Sue died, a part of the music industry died. Music Row will never be like it was when she was there. She was one of the finest people I've ever known," Waylon said.

Waylon conceived the TV project, phoned all the singer/songwriters, and made sure each guest artist sent in a letter of confirmation. He feels especially close to the fund (administered by The Songwriters Guild), which assists new songwriters.

Waylon hosted, co-created, and co-produced the Brewer TV special. At the taping segment which took place at the Grand Ole Opry House he told the audience: "They have a bunch of cue cards they want me to read. But guess what — I'm not going to. This show means too much to me to try to read for it" (*Nashville Banner*, October 11, 1984). Waylon was happy to learn that by early 1985 the Sue Brewer

Fund had already helped forty-two songwriters by granting then free time at one of a number of participating Nashville recording studios.

"Waylon's definitely happier than ever," his brother Tommy said in early 1985. "Basically, Waylon has never been nothin' intentionally but a gentleman and a damn good guy. We all leave footprints as we go, but you could stamp his 'I didn't mean to' if he didn't go in the right place.

"He treaded water—as long as they could make it rain."

Waylon recently recorded a song Tommy wrote called "Me and Them Three Brothers," which is filled with references to the Jennings' early days in Little-field, living on Austin Avenue, and working for a local freight company (which all four Jennings boys did).

One former member of road crew who asked not to be identified said of Waylon, "I always liked him—he's a nice man. His is a tough position to be in. He's surrounded by people who are not pleasant. He still has some losers around him."

Johanna Yurcic, Waylon's former road manager, said, "Waylon's made one hell of a musical statement. He just went a little too far in a few areas. . . . He brought about a lot of changes in the country music industry, no matter how he did it. Musically, I still think Waylon has one of the best voices there's ever been in country music."

A former RCA executive is glad to see Waylon off drugs, but isn't happy with the material Waylon has been releasing. "The stuff Waylon is doing now reminds me of an album he did years ago where he sounded like he was trying to croon like Sinatra," he said. "I can't tell if he's lost some of his voice, because he's singing bad songs. Let me hear him sing

'Are You Sure Hank Done It This Way' and I'll tell you whether he's still got his voice."

Waylon hasn't beaten the machine, of course — it's still there, and it will outlast him and every other country artist. But he is still a sign of encouragement to newcomers in all fields, artists who want to try things their own way.

"I'll never be completely contented. If that happens, it's all over. Time to go to sleep. . . . I don't have goals. . . . 'Cause you reach 'em, and then what? You're a success when you have a good mate and you get to do what you want to do to make a living. I'd consider myself lucky" (Dallas *Times Herald*, November 13, 1983).

When asked by interviewers about his plans for the future, throughout the years Waylon has replied with much the same answer: "I plan to finish this cigarette and go out on stage" . . . "I plan to finish these pistachios and go out on stage" . . . and so on, making it clear that he takes life as it comes.

"Really, my biggest goal is pretty simple. I'd just like to be remembered as a good person — someone who tried to help other people when they deserved it, and someone who had the courage to at least try and do things his own way. In those two categories, I'd just like to be remembered as having done the best I could" (*Genesis*, December 1984).

Country music has moved toward Waylon, not vice versa. Listen to the sax that Don Williams included on a recent hit, or the synthesizers that Dolly Parton often features on her tracks. Lee Greenwood's years of working Vegas lounges show in every recording he makes, and Kenny Rogers is as likely to record a duet with Sheena Easton as he is with Dottie West. For some country artists things are a whole lot more open than they were twenty years ago, due in some measure to Waylon's earlier career struggles.

While the Nashville music scene continues to work in the tension between modernists and traditionalists, the borders between various styles of country music have blurred. The recent golden age of country music, which benefitted from the popularity that followed the *Urban Cowboy* movie, appears to be fading, and record sales and concert bookings are far off their levels of a few years ago.

Waylon points out how Nashville exerted its pressure on Texas swing great Bob Wills (the Grand Ole Opry attempted to prevent Wills from using drums during his Opry performance), but the town now worships Wills in the Country Music Hall of Fame. "Now, tomorrow, if I died or was killed," Waylon said, "there'd be a rush to claim their own. Once you're out of their hair, you're beloved. Y'know, the 'late, great,' and 'what he did for our music.'

"But until then, it's always 'trouble-makin'-son-of-a-bitch' " (*Houston Chronicle*, September 7, 1975).

How would Waylon like to be thought of today? As he told the *Minneapolis Star* (June 6, 1980), "I'm Waylon Jennings. I'm a good ol' boy, as good as the best, as bad as the worst. And I like to sing."

APPENDICES

A. Selected Discographies: Waylon Jennings and Jessi Colter

Waylon Jennings Discography

Singles

1959 "Jole Blon," Brunswick

1961 "Another Blue Day," Trend '61

1963 "My Baby Walks All Over Me," Trend '63

1964 "Love Denied"/"Rave On," A&M

1964 "Four Strong Winds"/"Just to Satisfy You," A&M

1964 "Sing the Girls a Song Bill"/"The Race Is On," A&M

1965 "I Don't Believe You"/"The Real House of the Rising Sun," A&M

1965 "That's the Chance I'll Have to Take," RCA

1965 "Stop the World (And Let Me Off)," RCA

1966 "Anita, You're Dreaming," RCA

1966 "Time to Bum Again," RCA

1966 "That's What You Get for Loving Me," RCA

1966 "Green River," RCA

1967 "Mental Revenge," RCA

1967 "Chokin' Kind," RCA

1967 "Love of the Common People," RCA

1968 "Walk on Out of My Mind," RCA

1968 "I Got You" (with Anita Carter), RCA

1968 "Only Daddy That'll Walk the Line," RCA

1968 "Love of the Common People," RCA

1968 "Yours Love," RCA

1969 "Something's Wrong in California," RCA

1969 "The Days of Sand and Shovels," RCA

1969 "Delia's Gone," RCA

1969 "MacArthur Park" (with the Kimberleys), RCA

1969 "Brown-Eyed Handsome Man," RCA

1970 "Singer of Sad Songs," RCA

1970 "The Taker," RCA

1970 "Suspicious Minds" (with Jessi Colter), RCA

1970 "Don't Let the Sun Set on You in Tulsa," RCA

1971 "Mississippi Woman," RCA

1971 "Under Your Spell Again" (with Jessi Colter), RCA

1971 "Cedartown, Georgia," RCA

1972 "Good Hearted Woman," RCA

1972 "Sweet Dream Woman," RCA

1972 "Pretend I Never Happened," RCA

1973 "You Can Have Her," RCA

1973 "We Had It All," RCA

1973 "You Ask Me To," RCA

1974 "This Time," RCA

1974 "I'm a Ramblin' Man," RCA

1974 "Rainy Day Woman"/"Let's All Help the Cowboys Sing the Blues," RCA

1975 "Dreaming My Dreams With You," RCA

1975 "Are You Sure Hank Done It This Way"/"Bob Wills Is Still the King," RCA

1976 "Good Hearted Woman" (with Willie Nelson), RCA

1976 "Suspicious Minds" (with Jessi Colter) reissue, RCA

1976 "Can't You See"/"I'll Go Back to Her," RCA

1976 "Are You Ready for the Country," RCA

1977 "Luckenbach, Texas (Back to the Basics of Love)" (with Willie Nelson), RCA

1977 "The Wurlitzer Prize (I Don't Want to Get Over You)," RCA

1978 "Mammas Don't Let Your Babies Grow Up to Be Cowboys" (with Willie Nelson), RCA

1978 "There Ain't No Good Chain Gang" (with Johnny Cash), Columbia

1978 "I've Always Been Crazy," RCA

1978 "Don't You Think This Outlaw Bit's Done Got Out of Hand," RCA

1979 "Amanda," RCA

1979 "Come With Me," RCA

1980 "I Ain't Living Long Like This," RCA

1980 "Clyde," RCA

1980 "Theme From the Dukes of Hazzard (Good Ol' Boys)," RCA

1981 "Storms Never Last" (with Jessi Colter), RCA

1981 "It Wasn't God Who Made Honky Tonk Angels/Wild Side of Life (medley)" (with Jessi Colter), RCA

1981 "Shine," RCA

1982 "Just to Satisfy You" (with Willie Nelson), RCA

1982 "Women Do Know How To Carry On," RCA

1982 "(Sittin' on) The Dock of the Bay" (with Willie Nelson), RCA

1983 "Lucille (You Won't Do Your Daddy's Will)," RCA

1983 "Breakin' Down," RCA

1983 "Hold On, I'm Comin' " (with Jerry Reed), RCA

1983 "The Conversation" (with Hank Williams, Jr.), RCA

1983 "Take It To the Limit," Columbia (with Willie Nelson)

1984 "I May Be Used (But Baby I Ain't Used Up)," RCA

1984 "Never Could Toe the Mark," RCA

1985 "America," RCA

1985 "Waltz Me to Heaven," RCA

1985 "Drinkin' and Dreamin'," RCA

Albums (Waylon Jennings)

1964 *Waylon Jennings at J.D.'s*, Sound Limited

1966 *Folk-Country*, RCA

1966 *Leavin' Town*, RCA

1966 *Nashville Rebel*, RCA

1967 *Waylon Sings Ol' Harlan*, RCA

1967 *Love of the Common People*, RCA

1967 *The One and Only Waylon Jennings*, RCA

1968 *Hangin' On*, RCA

1968 *Only the Greatest*, RCA

1968 *Jewels*, RCA

1969 *Just to Satisfy You*, RCA

1969 *Waylon Jennings*, Vocalion (tracks from *J.D.'s* album)

1970 *Country Folk: Waylon Jennings and the Kimberleys*, RCA

1970 *Waylon*, RCA

1970 *Don't Think Twice*, RCA

1970 *Jessi Colter: A Country Star Is Born*, RCA (Waylon co-produced, and sings backup)

1970 *The Best of Waylon Jennings*, RCA

1970 *Ned Kelly*, United Artists (movie soundtrack)

1970 *Singer of Sad Songs*, RCA

1971 *The Taker/Tulsa*, RCA

1971 *Cedartown, Georgia*, RCA

1972 *Good Hearted Woman*, RCA

1972 *Heartaches By the Number*, RCA

1972 *Ladies Love Outlaws*, RCA

1973 *Ruby, Don't Take Your Love to Town*, Camden

1973 *Lonesome, On'ry and Mean*, RCA

1973 *Honky Tonk Heroes*, RCA

1974 *This Time*, RCA

1974 *Only Daddy That'll Walk the Line*, Camden

1974 *Waylon, the Ramblin' Man*, RCA

1975 *Dreaming My Dreams*, RCA

1976 *Wanted! The Outlaws* (with Willie Nelson, Jessi Colter, and Tompall Glaser), RCA

1976 *MacIntosh and T.J.*, RCA (movie soundtrack)

1976 *Are You Ready for the Country*, RCA

1976 *The Dark Side of Fame*, Camden (reissue of 1967's *The One and Only Waylon Jennings*)

1976 *Waylon—Live*, RCA

1977 *Ol' Waylon*, RCA

1978 *Waylon and Willie* (with Willie Nelson), RCA

1978 *I Would Like to See You Again*, Columbia (Waylon sings on this Johnny Cash album)

1978 *White Mansions*, A&M (with other artists)

1978 *I've Always Been Crazy*, RCA

1979 *Greatest Hits*, RCA

1979 *What Goes Around Comes Around*, RCA

1979 *George Jones and Friends*, Epic (Waylon sings on this LP)

1980 *Music Man*, RCA
1981 *Leather and Lace* (with Jessi Colter), RCA
1982 *Black on Black*, RCA
1982 *WWII*, RCA
1983 *Take It to the Limit* (with Willie Nelson), Columbia
1983 *It's Only Rock and Roll*, RCA
1983 *Waylon and Company*, RCA
1984 *Never Could Toe the Mark*, RCA
1984 *Waylon's Greatest Hits Vol. 2*, RCA
1985 *The Highwayman* (with Willie Nelson, Johnny Cash, and Kris Kristofferson), Columbia
1985 *Turn the Page*, RCA

Jessi Colter Discography

Singles

1970 "Suspicious Minds" (with Waylon Jennings), RCA
1971 "Under Your Spell Again" (with Waylon Jennings), RCA
1975 "I'm Not Lisa," Capitol
1975 "What's Happened to Blue Eyes"/"You Ain't Never Been Loved (Like I'm Gonna Love You)," Capitol
1976 "It's Morning (And I Still Love You)," Capitol
1976 "Without You," Capitol
1976 "Suspicious Minds" (reissue) (with Waylon Jennings), RCA
1976 "I Thought I Heard You Calling My Name," Capitol
1977 "I Belong to Him," Capitol
1978 "Maybc You Should've Been Listening," Capitol
1979 "Love Me Back to Sleep," Capitol
1981 "Storms Never Last" (with Waylon Jennings), RCA
1981 "Wild Side of Life/It Wasn't God Who Made Honky Tonk Angels (medley)" (with Waylon Jennings), RCA
1982 "Holdin' On," Capitol

Albums

1970 *A Country Star Is Born*, RCA
1975 *I'm Jessi Colter*, Capitol
1976 *Jessi*, Capitol
1976 *Diamond in the Rough*, Capitol
1977 *Mirriam*, Capitol
1978 *That's the Way a Cowboy Rocks and Rolls*, Capitol
1981 *Leather and Lace*, (with Waylon Jennings), RCA

B. Top Songs: Waylon Jennings

Number-One Songs in Billboard *magazine:*

1974 "This Time"
1974 "I'm A Ramblin' Man"
1975 "Are You Sure Hank Done It This Way"
1975 "Good Hearted Woman" (with Willie Nelson)
1977 "Luckenbach, Texas (Back to the Basics of Love)" (with Willie Nelson)
1977 "Wurlitzer Prize"
1978 "I've Always Been Crazy"
1978 "Mammas Don't Let Your Babies Grow Up to be Cowboys" (with Willie Nelson)
1979 "Amanda"
1979 "Come With Me"
1980 "Ain't Living Long Like This"
1980 "Theme From the Dukes of Hazzard (Good Ol' Boys)"
1982 "Just to Satisfy You" (with Willie Nelson)
1983 "Lucille"

BMI (Broadcast Music, Inc.) Award Winning Songs
(for airplay, with year award was given):

1972, 1976, 1977 "Good Hearted Woman"
1974 "You Ask Me To"
1975 "This Time"
1976 "Are You Sure Hank Done It This Way"
1976 "Rainy Day Woman"
1979 "I've Always Been Crazy"
1980, 1981 "Theme From the Dukes of Hazzard (Good Ol' Boys)"
1982 "Shine"
1982, 1983 "Just to Satisfy You"
1982, 1983 "Women Do Know How to Carry On"

C. Major Awards: Waylon Jennings

Country Music Association
(CMA Awards)

1975 Male Vocalist of the Year
1976 Single of the Year for "Good Hearted Woman" (with Willie Nelson)
1976 Album of the Year for *Wanted! The Outlaws* (with Willie Nelson, Jessi Colter, and Tompall Glaser)
1976 Vocal Duo of the Year (with Willie Nelson)

NARAS (National Academy of Recording Arts and Sciences)
(Grammy Awards)

1969 Best Country Performance by Duo or Group for "MacArthur Park" (with the Kimberleys)
1978 Best Country Performance by Duo or Group for "Mamas Don't Let Your Babies Grow Up to Be Cowboys" (with Willie Nelson)

D. Gold and Platinum Waylon Jennings Records*
Album   Certification
(Year of Release)

Album (Year of Release)	Certification
Dreaming My Dreams (1975)	gold
Wanted! The Outlaws (1976) (with Willie Nelson, Tompall Glaser, and Jessi Colter)	double platinum
Are You Ready for the Country (1976)	gold
Waylon—Live (1976)	gold
Ol' Waylon (1977)	platinum
Waylon & Willie (1978) (with Willie Nelson)	double platinum
I've Always Been Crazy (1978)	platinum
Greatest Hits (1979)	quadruple platinum
What Goes Around Comes Around (1979)	gold
Music Man (1980)	gold
Leather and Lace (1982) (with Jessi Colter)	gold
WWII (1982) (with Willie Nelson)	gold

*gold = 500,000
  units sold
 platinum = 1,000,000
  units sold

Single (Year of Release)	Certification
"Theme From the Dukes of Hazzard (Good Ol' Boys)" (1980)	platinum

*gold = one million
    units sold
 platinum = two million
    units sold

THESE ZEBRA MYSTERIES
ARE SURE TO KEEP
YOU GUESSING

By Sax Rohmer

THE DRUMS OF FU MANCHU	(1617, $3.50)
THE TRAIL OF FU MANCHU	(1619, $3.50)
THE INSIDIOUS DR. FU MANCHU	(1668, $3.50)

By Mary Roberts Rinehart

THE HAUNTED LADY	(1685, $3.50)
THE SWIMMING POOL	(1686, $3.50)

By Ellery Queen

WHAT'S IN THE DARK	(1648, $2.95)

Available wherever paperbacks are sold, or order direct from the Publisher. Send cover price plus 50¢ per copy for mailing and handling to Zebra Books, Dept. 1722, 475 Park Avenue South, New York, N.Y. 10016. DO NOT SEND CASH.